BOA
EDITIONS LTD

AN ORCHARD IN THE STREET

AN ORCHARD IN THE STREET

STORIES BY

REGINALD GIBBONS

AMERICAN READER SERIES, No. 29

BOA EDITIONS, LTD. ～ ROCHESTER, NY ～ 2017

First Edition
17 18 19 20   7 6 5 4 3 2 1

For information about permission to reuse any material from this book please
contact The Permissions Company at www.permissionscompany.com or e-mail
permdude@gmail.com.

Publications by BOA Editions, Ltd.—a not-for-profit cor-
poration under section 501 (c) (3) of the United States
Internal Revenue Code—are made possible with funds from
a variety of sources, including public funds from the Litera-
ture Program of the National Endowment for the Arts; the
New York State Council on the Arts, a state agency; and the
County of Monroe, NY. Private funding sources include the
Lannan Foundation for support of the Lannan Translations
Selection Series; the Max and Marian Farash Charitable
Foundation; the Mary S. Mulligan Charitable Trust; the
Rochester Area Community Foundation; the Steeple-Jack Fund; the Ames-
Amzalak Memorial Trust in memory of Henry Ames, Semon Amzalak, and Dan
Amzalak; and contributions from many individuals nationwide. See Colophon
on page 132 for special individual acknowledgments.

ART WORKS.
arts.gov

State of the Arts

NYSCA

Cover Art: *Man with a Gun* by Tony Fitzpatrick
Cover Design: Sandy Knight
Interior Design and Composition: Richard Foerster
Manufacturing: McNaughton & Gunn
BOA Logo: Mirko

Library of Congress Cataloging-in-Publication Data

Names: Gibbons, Reginald, author.
Title: An orchard in the street / Reginald Gibbons.
Description: First edition. | Rochester, NY : BOA Editions Ltd., 2017. |
  Series: American readers series ; no. 29
Identifiers: LCCN 2017014732 (print) | LCCN 2017021308 (ebook) | ISBN
  9781942683506 (eBook) | ISBN 9781942683490 (softcover)
Subjects: | BISAC: FICTION / Short Stories (single author). | FICTION /
  Literary. | FICTION / Visionary & Metaphysical. | LITERARY COLLECTIONS /
  American / General.
Classification: LCC PS3557.I1392 (ebook) | LCC PS3557.I1392 A6 2017 (print)
  |
  DDC 813/.54—dc23
LC record available at https://lccn.loc.gov/2017014732

BOA Editions, Ltd.
250 North Goodman Street, Suite 306
Rochester, NY 14607
www.boaeditions.org
A. Poulin, Jr., Founder (1938–1996)

remembering W. R. G. and W. G.

. . . to bind up the brokenhearted,
to proclaim liberty to the captives,
and the opening of the prison
to them that are bound.

—Isaiah 61:1

Contents

River

Stay in the river, Bill was told by Father John. "Stay in the river, don't go over to the bank and climb up there into those weeds, stay out in the middle, go where it's flowing. You don't *know* where it's flowing but you have to stay in it, you don't have to know, you can't know. Stay in the river."

"But," Bill said, "I've been around rivers and streams all my life, I've been up in those weeds and found those fantastic nests in there, with all those eggs, those wonderful nests, that's where I like to be."

"But that's only till they hatch. That's only for them to leave, so they can get into the river, even the mama leaves that nest as soon as she can with those offspring of hers, or she's got the kind that she can leave them, on the right day, and she goes back into the river—no, you can't stay there . . . Stay in the river, don't be afraid of where it's going to carry you, that's where you're meant to be."

Mekong Restaurant, 1986

What's the half-life of a city?

Elsewhere, far away, green shoots of rice as new as creation, a soft harmless color, rippling, shimmering, in a breeze over the flat surface of water, outside a village of frail huts with talk in them, under trees of a green hot place drenched by rain, in a country of rain clouds and smoke clouds and fire clouds.

A menu in Vietnamese and English.

A dozen immigrants waiting among native and naturalized citizens for their boxes and bags inside a terminal at O'Hare. Refugees streamed back the way that long war had come to them—into the very country that had turned guns and poured fire on them. The immigrants have brought their children and their names with them. Some of their children; some of their parents and uncles and aunts; names that must struggle to be pronounced inside unfamiliar mouths.

But along these streets ice-winds race. And in summer the raw weedy vacant lots show a jewel glitter sparkling like sequins on fields of ragged green and crumbly gray—innumerable bits of shattered glass under the half-open windows of apartment buildings and ramshackle three-flats, a few with new paint and siding. Up and down the busy street there are shops—

Viet Hoa Market, Nha Trang Restaurant, Video King, White Hen, Viet Mien Restaurant, McDonalds, Dr. Ngo Phung Dentist, Nguyen Quang Attorney at Law, Viet My Department Store, Casino Tours. High and far as mountains beyond and above the roofs of this street the winter gray-on-white cityscape wears banners of steam flapping straight sideways in the bitter wind. If you stare at the big buildings long enough you might begin to sense a foundational anxiety in the balanced masses of stone and you might wonder why they don't just fall. Fall!

Go out into a vacant lot, or even into a park, and hide under a weed.

Same moon. Not the same moon. After danger and escapes, after straining so intensely to survive—living in this place makes some feel they have come to their own funeral. To live away from your own place, far away, and to think you will never return, is to be condemned to have been saved one time too many, some will feel. When meteor showers fall in winter and summer you won't see them because the underbelly of the sky is lit orange all night in every season. But the children grow accustomed.

An immigrant boy of fourteen wearing black trousers and a white shirt and a thin jacket is standing with his immigrant parents at the counter of the high-school office, waiting to be called in to be registered; the two clerks are busy, giving the immigrants only a glance, and the mother and father and boy are waiting. At this school the students speak twenty-nine languages, or forty-one, or sixty-three.

The year lasts longer here. It's a proven fact of quantum longing—that time passes more slowly when the air is cold than when it is warm, and that snow and bright streetlights are emotionally radioactive. Not so far away is a famous atom smasher that generates twirling nanosecond particles, and around itself it pays for wide reaches of lovely restored native prairie.

In this place are two zoos, many banks, millions of persons, and the inland sea, frozen this year near the shore, and perhaps for the last time in years to come. From wave water splashed into the air, where it freezes, crumbly hills of ice have risen along the beaches, and beside the lakefront roads blackened piles and heaps of soft-hard decayed slush. The fast traffic rolls and rolls.

A menu in English and Vietnamese.

It's late, he's looking out through the kitchen pickup window at three American strangers, still in their overcoats, who have come in, who are looking around, who are sitting down at a table.

What is the half-life of a city?

Five Pears or Peaches

Buckled into the cramped back seat, she sings to herself
as I drive toward her school through the town streets.
Straining upward to see out her window, she watches
the things that go by, the ones she sees—I know only
that some of them are the houses we sometimes say
we wish were ours. But today as we pass them we only
think it; or I do, while she's singing—the big yellow
one with a roofed portico for cars never there, the red-
shuttered pink stucco one that's her favorite. Most of
what she sings rhymes as it unwinds in the direction she
goes with it. Half the way to school she sings, and then
she stops, the song becomes something she'd rather
keep to herself, the underground sweet-water stream
through the tiny continent of her, on which her high
oboe voice floats through forests softly, the calling of
a hidden pensive bird—this is how I strain my grasp to
imagine what it's like for her to be thinking of things,
to herself, to be feeling her happiness or fear.

  After I leave her inside the small school, which
was converted from an old house in whose kitchen you
can almost still smell the fruit being cooked down for
canning, she waves goodbye from a window, and I can
make her cover her mouth with one hand and laugh
and roll her eyes at a small classmate if I cavort a little

down the walk.

In some of her paintings, the sun's red and has teeth, but the houses are cheerful, and fat flying birds with almost human faces and long noses for beaks sail downward toward the earth, where her giant bright flowers overshadow like trees the people she draws.

When the day is ending, her naked delight in the bath is delight in a lake of still pleasures, a straight un-hurried sailing in a good breeze, and a luxurious trust that there will always be this calm warm weather, and someone's hand to steer and steady the skiff of her. Ashore, orchards are blooming.

Before I get into bed with her mother at night, in our own house, I look in on her and watch her sleeping hands come near her face to sweep away what's bother-ing her dreaming eyes. I ease my hand under her back and lift her from the edge of the bed to the center. I can almost catch the whole span of her shoulders in one hand—five pears or peaches, it might be, dreaming in a delicate basket—till they tip with their own live weight and slip from my grasp.

Wonder

Along the dark neighborhood sidewalk, a casual, brazen raccoon waddling toward the nearby moonlit limitless lake seems to expect me to stand out of its way. I certainly do. More sightings of the other residents of this lakeshore plain have marked the meanwhile tumultuous human seasons—a running, frightened, confused deer clattering its small hooves down our street of shy silent houses early on a Sunday morning, far from any woods; a red fox that trotted out of a scraggly hedge and across my path as I was walking; in a tall bush beside our trash can, a transient gorgeous warbler lit by a shaft of sunlight on a windy, cloudy morning; and one bright afternoon when inside the house I heard for half an hour a faraway continuous honking of Canada geese. Finally I went outside to see how there could be so many. I looked up through the sunlit limitless spring sky at endless interconnected irregular skeins of them, so far up, V and V and V and V branching again and again from each other, thousands and thousands of geese, honking en masse to make their ceaseless goose and gander music, and amazingly, crossing the whole sky, the sky from church roof to treetops and house chimneys. Their calls were resounding even inside the neighborhoods' hot dusty attics, alleyway garages, basements. Fifty thousand flying geese, a hundred thousand, how many? In the small gravel parking lot of the old red-brick church, four neighbors and I stood with heads back, not speaking, watching the geese wavily pattern the whole sky the same way waves pattern the lake, until after we had watched together for twenty minutes, that immense, inconceivable effort of birds was more than our minds could reach toward any more; it pushed our imaginations aside, it exhausted our attention, it tired our feeble necks, it would never happen again where we could see it, it was like a mythical visitation that human beings were meant to witness for the sake of a cleansing of the spirit. Rippling lines drawn across the whole sky by beating wings.

Bless This House

It's late morning, and inside one of the small houses standing always side by side up and down the street, there is quiet. All three beds have been left unmade upstairs, dirty dishes from the night before lie in the kitchen sink, two damp clumped towels lie on the floor of the one bathroom, downstairs, and the front door has locked something in—the daytime absence that no one can ever witness. They all rushed out—he for the whole day, she and the children for her errands and their doctor and then the supermarket, and the children would get sweets to soothe the shock of the needles.

Before this, before the rush to leave, even before anyone awoke, what was there? There was peace in the small rooms on the second floor. Into each of the four dreaming souls the sounds of the spring daylight had begun to enter: the chirping town birds in trees and bushes—robins, sparrows, and a triumphant cardinal shouting from somewhere—and the first few cars starting, and an early plane too high up to be heard.

Before that, in the half-sleeping night, lying in bed face to face, the man and woman with closed eyes had lain still, aware along their bodies of each other's warmth and solidity in the dimness—exhausted, remedyless, greedy for at least the least contentment of having gone past the time for work or thought, lying half asleep in the half comfort of each other's arms.

Before that, before anyone had gone to bed, there was the sound of their younger child crying. The father held the little girl awhile, whisper-singing off-key, "Hush little baby, don't say a word, Daddy's gonna buy you . . ." It didn't work, and back in her crib the little one cried and cried, softly, and also called a few times so achingly that when at last she stopped and was calm, not yet helped but too tired to keep crying, there came from next door the sound of another child crying, child who had heard her call and was relaying it on, unable not to, renewing the search for an answer that sometimes is known to no parent.

Before that, it had been bedtime—some separate sorrow twisting the face of the boy, older by three years, wringing a few tears from him too. An obsessing heart might falter at such seemingly helpless sadness. But it passed through him and went away somewhere and shyly he came back to them and sat close to his mother on the couch, happier again. And the mother's shoulders were no longer, for a while, too heavy, the father stood less pained and weak, less in danger of becoming angry, his face not failing him or his family.

Before that, there had been television, and before that, dessert, and before that, dinner. All the while the little boy was feeling something he didn't want to feel, something as scratchy as wool in his being and he ran here and there and made noise and poked his infant sister with his finger and upset her and then gave his trouble to his mother. She took it from him wearily, but the man and the woman did not know anything about what troubled him, and the boy couldn't say it because he couldn't quite think it.

Before that, there had been the man's arrival home, relieved, tired, looking as if some of his very substance had been worn from him again by the day's work. Wanting to be restored by his children but having to try to help restore them and their mother. Hadn't each of them too flowed like water through the unique and ordinary day and arrived again at a place never before known—this late afternoon, this moment? In the aisles of supermarkets, one after another, the man had stood, with one painful foot in a shoe half unlaced, he rested that foot on edge, his hand marked the long sheets on his clipboard, his eyes counted things and things, his hands neatened the stock he had delivered—the soft loaves of bread in their soft plastic sleeves, the packaged muffins . . . In a slow hurry . . .

At his entrance into the realm of the woman and the two children, he had put on some cheer for them, and lifted both children up, one in each arm, and hugged them, and felt the precious hands of the little boy at the back of his cricked neck and in his grateful hair, the adorable heft and scent of the tiny girl. And he had remembered to ask what he could of the woman's day and he had tried to listen to her and he had thought of a dozen things he would have liked to tell her if he could have found the words, if long before now he had found them, so that they would have been ready when he needed them. But he was home, the day had taken him from himself and even now kept him from them, somewhat. It was too late, at this passing moment, to find the words. And could he hope that she would care to hear him beyond her own cares, which also weighed on him?

Before that, the woman had tried to hold her back just so—there was a little catch in it that had been jabbing her with pain for four days if she didn't hold herself just so. She thought about how to speak to the man, about what to say, what to ask, how to ask it, how to hope he would answer it, how to make a beginning of a beginning of a change, how to figure out what it was that could be changed, that needed to be changed, how to change it, how to find a place to start, inside these rooms, clothes, hopes. How to hold on, to live each date of the calendar in what seemed the endless succession of days of attending to the children and everything that had to be done. Find the corner where the dissonance sounded, when it did, and go there and smooth it—how to do that, how to find whatever it was that was not what it should be, whatever it was they wanted, the two of them, the mingled commitments that together they lived but that seemed to be almost entirely hers alone to feed and warm and prod into speech—that simple overwhelming *how*. And wanting, needing, to wait two years more before leaving both children in some stranger's arms and care.

Before that, on the small round table in their bedroom, in a quiet moment of the day when woman and children had all been elsewhere, a small, faded, sentimental cloth had lain flat where it had been carefully smoothed for a lamp and a book, had hung irregularly over the edge a few inches all around, its grapes and leaves and red border motionless. The lamp's yellow burlap shade insisted on a mood of cheer; and the book had been left in an artful posture, to one side, awaiting a charmed kiss of attention that in some way was mutual and would at the same moment be felt by the woman—whose hand, a few days earlier, had left it there with a tiny unspoken hope. Had lingered over leaving it there.

She needed a moment to reach back, to touch lightly—as you might touch the leaf of a houseplant after you had watered it with generosity and helpfulness in your spirit—what had been, to make it grow in just a slightly different direction, somehow, for the sake of a morning that would come spilling light on what simply is, confirming it—it in all its unrecoverable unknowing preparations.

The stillness, the absence, the current of the days, the space in which everything that happened and everything that didn't happen became the story. Every moment creating the next out of itself and looking back to how it had come to be, how it was filled by the four of them, how it could never disclose to them why at some hours its emptiness was filled with what it could not say.

The Vanishing Point

A young man with very bad teeth and a walleyed gaze, holding some poster boards on his lap, where they sagged on each side, and drawing on the top one with an old, chewed, blue-ink ballpoint pen. It was a severely rectilinear highway scene: a powerful exaggerated vanishing point puckering the empty horizon, lanes of cars coming on—as yet only outlined—and lanes of big trucks going away, already finished. One after another, all alike, semitrailers with company names on them, and all the wording and perspective acutely correct. It all looked to have been drawn with a ruler, strictly and slowly, but he was doing it freehand—each stroke of his pen absolutely precise. Or rather, as imprecise as the human hand, but with an authority that could convey and even create his precision in your own eyes as you watched. The lettering he was putting on the side of the last, closest, largest trailer was as if painted by machine, and he never paused to consider proportions or angles but simply kept drawing and darkening the shapes with the cheap ink, as if rapidly tracing not drawing a faint design that was already there on the white floppy board.

This was at Chicago and State, in the subway station.

A pale woman happened to come stand near him, and watched as he worked with his intent rhythm, his head bobbing and sometimes with his dark face low to study his work closely with one eye at a time. She watched, and he noticed her and smiled a wrecked-tooth wide sort of blindman's smile at her, and said, more than asked, "Nice work, idn't it?" She put her right thumb up and smiled back at him, and said nothing, and he lifted the top board and showed her the finished one underneath, for an instant—another roadscape, in several colors, filled in and alive, the whole huge white board crammed with convincing and convinced detail.

"Nice work, idn't it!" he said again, and showed her the one underneath that one. Again, thumb up, and she too smiled happily—a wholly natural acknowledgment of him, an unsurprised understanding of his talent. She didn't act as if it seemed strange to her that he was sitting on a worn drab bench on the subway platform, next to the tracks, working in the dim light while commuters and others stood around waiting impatiently for the next train. It didn't seem to strike her as out of the usual that he was half-blind and so intensely at his work. That his work was driven, obsessively scrupulous, uninhabited, repetitive, brilliant, rhythmical, depthless, spiritless, useless.

"Nice work, idn't it!" he said to her each time, and he showed her—and me, because I too was standing there—six or eight more drawings: the hundred-and-eight-story tower, the skyline along Michigan Avenue, the traffic in the streets, not a single person. The long lines were perfectly smooth and straight but when you looked at them more closely you saw that they zigged with freehand force across the board in short spurts. And her thumb went up to each in turn, and she smiled and each time she did, he said, "Nice work, idn't it!"

"I do nice work!" he said. "I did *all* these, and not a *single mistake*! Nice work!" he was saying as the train came in like sandpaper, hissing and braking. She walked away toward it without saying goodbye, and he looked at me, then. "Nice work, idn't it!" he said, as cheerfully as a man could ever say it.

"It's beautiful!" I said. The doors of the train opened a few feet away, everyone was crowding inside, and I stepped in, the great force in him still holding me, and with part of myself I wished it would win—for my sake, not his—but I had gotten in, the last passenger, "It's nice *work*!" he said to me, smiling, nodding, and the doors slid shut and immediately the train jerked and began to roll out of the station and away.

No Matter What Has Happened This May

I love the little row of life along the low rusted
garden-wire fence that divides my small city backyard
from my neighbor's. The wild unruly rose, I hacked
like a weed last spring; then it shot quick running
lengths of vine in every direction and shuddered into
a thickness of blown blossoms—the kind you can't cut
and take in because they fall apart. The violets, just
beautiful weeds. Then there are yellow-green horse-
radish leaves—they rose as fast as dandelions in today's rain and then sun. And the oregano and mint
are coming back, too—you can't discourage them.
Last year's dry raspberry canes are leaning, caught
in the thorns of the new, at the corner. And beyond
them, the mostly gone magnolia in the widow's yard,
behind ours, the white petals on the ground in a circle like a crocheted bedspread thrown down around
the black trunk.

I went out to see what the end of the day was like,
away from everything for a minute, and again a few
drops of rain were falling. I touched the ground, just
to feel the wet of it against my palm; and the old side
of the house, too. In the quiet, I saw two robins bring-
ing weeds and twigs to a nesting place hidden in the
new leaves at the stumpy top of a trimmed limb of the

buckeye. How little they need—weeds and some time—
to build with.

In a month I may find a new one not yet fully fledged,
lost from the nest, and I may put it on the highest limb
I can reach, but not high enough to escape harm's way,
I imagine, when the harm is the shock within it after
its disastrous fall, and it may be dead before morning.
That's happened before. But these robins were just now
building, and one came with a full beak and paused a
moment on a lower branch and cocked its head and
looked upward and shifted its feet and then leapt up
and disappeared into the buckeye leaves, as the single
drops of rain were gently shaking them one by one,
here and there. Nearby somewhere, singing, a cricket.

I was getting wet but I felt held outside because I
could hear, from inside our house, a woman and small
child—wife and daughter—laughing in the bathtub
together, their laughter not meant for me but brought
out to me like a gift by the damp still air. I could see
that like the rain and the robins and the weeds and
roses and raspberry canes they too were working and
building. I'm not going to mention now any harm or
hurt they have suffered. No winter or summer pain,
no wounded persons or trees, no small figures fallen.
I wiped the wet and dirt off my palms and I picked up
again the glass of wine I had carried out with me. I
rejoiced. There was no way not to, with the sound of
that laughter and whispering in the last light of a day
we had lived.

Money

The three children are eating lunch in the kitchen on a summer weekday when a man comes to the latched screen side door and knocks and they hear him ask their mother if she has anything that needs fixing or carrying or any yardwork he can do. They chew their sandwiches a little dreamily as she says, with her back straight and her voice carefully polite, No thank you, I'm sorry, and the man goes away. Who was that, Mama? they say. No one, she says.

They are sitting down to dinner but they have to wait because the doorbell rings and their father looks out the small round window in the old brown front door and then opens it and they see a thin young boy with a strong voice who begins to tell about a Sales Program he's completing for a Scholarship to be Supervisor, and he holds up a smudged, worn, tattered little booklet. The children do not perceive his novice guile and in-eradicable hope. Their father says, No thank you, Sorry but I can't help you out this time, Good luck. The boy goes away. The children start to eat and don't ask any-thing, because the boy was just a boy, but when their father sits down again he acts irritated and hasty.

Once, a glassy-eyed heavy girl who almost seems asleep as she stands under the front porch light on a warm night in autumn and offers for sale some little hand towels stitched by the blind people at the Lighthouse for the Blind and all three children, hiding just a little in the folds of their mother's full skirt, listen to the girl's high voice and their mother says, Well, I bought some the last time, but I can't do it this time.

She buys the children school supplies and food, she pays the two boys for mowing the yard together and weeding her flower beds. She gets a new sewing machine for her birthday from the children's father, and she buys new fabric and thread and patterns and makes dresses for the girls. Saving money. She patches the boy's cousin's hand-me-down shirts and jeans. She tells each of the children to put a dime or quarter from their allowance into the collection plate at church, and once a month she puts in a little sealed white envelope, and the ushers move slowly along the ends of the pews weaving the baskets through the congregation as the organist plays a long piece of music.

Look at it all—whisk brooms, magazine subscriptions, anything you need hauled away, Little League raffle tickets, chocolate candy, can I do any yardwork again and again, hairbrushes, Christmas cards, do you need help with your ironing one time, and more—they all came calling at the front door while the children were sometimes eating, sometimes playing. Their faces would soften with a kind of comfort in the authority of mother or father, with a kind of wonder at the needy callers.

Their father left for work every day early, and came home for dinner, and almost always went again on Saturday. In his car. Their mother drove them places in her car. She opened a savings account for each child and into each put the first five dollars. The children felt proud to see their names in the passbooks. They wanted to know when they could take the money out, but they were told they had to save their money, not spend it. In that long ago time they felt a kind of pleasure in these mysteries, to know that there were things you would understand later when you grew up and had your own house and while your own children were eating their dinner and making too much unwanted noise just as you had done, the doorbell would ring or there would come a knock-knock, the familiar surprise of it, who would it be, and someone would be holding a little worn book or a bundle of dishtowels or once an old man, but maybe he only looked so old, with his pale ragged beard, came with bunches of carnations, white, red, and pink. They didn't see, but look at him now as he walks slowly away still holding in both arms all his flowers.

Julius Johnson, 1995

The extraordinary night had ended, young Sharon Judith Ann (he loved her having three first names) had gone back into her house, and at five a.m. on Thursday young Julius Johnson, high-school senior, track and field, slipped back into his. His parents and his older sister were none the wiser, although they would have been astonished to know what had happened to their Julius, of whom they would never have predicted such triumph (as he felt it), or falling into sin (as they would have judged it). He lay down in his clothes and could not sleep, and an hour later, when his father, who rose before all others and showered, shaved and put on his work clothes and beat-up boots before the rest of the family even woke, called out Julius's name, Julius feigned a sleepy reply, behind his closed bedroom door, he feigned dressing quickly and he pulled the bedspread down and mussed the bed to make it look right. He never made his bed and his mother had given up on that long ago, and would make his bed after she got home from work. He heard his father call his sister's name. She was always almost late to her new job. He heard the usual sounds of morning in the house, but now he noticed them almost one by one, and he smelled the browned-butter scent of frying eggs. In a state of wonder and doubt, he entered the kitchen and sat down at the everyday table which seemed to him strange and incomprehensible, and he ate the eggs over easy and toast and bacon which his father had as always occupied himself with making, even on this incredible, unprecedented day, while Julius's sister, whom his father also served, was still in her nightgown, her head bent down, her hair unmanageable and her eyes presumably still closed against the unfair light of day. She ate in silence, even on this day! And Julius's mother with silent reverence immersed herself in preparing her own ritual coffee precisely as she wished it (even on this day!), although repeatedly she glanced at Julius, and seemed to catch his eye. But she said nothing. She too was a woman. Sharon Judith Ann was a woman. In his mind, Julius saw Sharon Judith Ann's extraordinary living creatureliness, her simple and stupefying nakedness. Julius's mother went on with her coffee-making and then her slow coffee-sipping, and lingered to communicate wordlessly to Julius an indulgent, protective, uninformed blessing. Then, answering the demands of her unswerving routine, by which she made life endurable in the face of meaninglessness and pillaging merciless time itself, she bore her coffee away to her bedroom where she would carefully dress for work, while Julius's father, after himself cleaning the kitchen in his quick efficient way, would matter-of-factly leave in his own car for the nowadays half-empty parking lot at the plant. Even on this day. Julius's mother, who had the good car, would soon be waiting impatiently for his sister to finish getting ready, and would quarrel with her as they walked out, and his sister would say very little, and the mother and daughter would enter the outer day of their crappy jobs, their disappointments and small triumphs, the satisfactions of being away from each other and the need to be with each other. Carrying a stuffed CD case and his old player, and some tattered notebooks and leaden textbooks in his high-school backpack, Julius was unable to say anything about himself to any of these blood kin with whom he had lived all his life. His friend would arrive soon in his beat-up car and drive them both to school. After school, Julius would pick up a javelin and ask himself what in the world it was, and would throw it not nearly as far as usual. Uncannily, offering her morning motto to him, Julius's mother had said, "Do what's right," and had smiled sadly at him, and then hugged him, and left, and a few minutes later the mute sister listlessly put her arms around Julius's shoulders and to his surprise kissed him on the cheek. Julius's sister, too, a woman.

From inside his friend's car, Julius looked back at the house in which he had grown up, feeling for an instant—but not acting on this feeling—that now that everyone else was gone, and he too was leaving, the house would divulge some incredible secret to him if only he would rush back inside and stand in the burned-butter-scented quiet. As the car rolled backwards down the short driveway into the street, Julius could hear the muted sound of the elderly next-door neighbor woman practicing her piano, as she often did in the early morning—a swirling music of interior dancing and dirging. Chopin, Julius's mother had told him.

What if without telling anyone he left home forever, and the whole town? (But how could he even think that? . . . Sharon Judith Ann.) By chance, by luck, by what made no sense, by design of God or the devil, Julius could, he *could*, he realized, do anything—he could for example disappear—he could take his first and only flight away from the realm of blood relations, of sudden school friendships and ruptures, of hyper raptures and hammer-stunned mute grief. Julius would not look down through the malevolent treacherous air, nor back in time, but would picture in his mind again, as innumerable times he had already pictured, images of some paradise of freedom from obligation, freedom from rain and rot, freedom from time—freedom from Fortune herself, even if She was laughing at the wheel she turned, to which everyone was bound. She too— Julius was thinking—a woman. Every minute in the air, Julius would watch his old world fall and fall away as the plane rose and rose. He would see images that he could not quite imagine now. At the end of the flight, at the end of his escape—he would return! He would return to his world to discover again what it was, and it could not but be the most changed place.

"Hey! Did you hear what I said?" his friend yelled at him. Julius slammed the creaking car door shut and the echo flew through the parking lot and seventeen streets. The two of them walked from the weather into the school. The halls were full of jostling and noise and smells of mops, dust, old metal, and armpits. Where was Sharon Judith Ann? Julius began to perceive in his extraordinariness the extraordinariness of everyone else's ordinariness, too.

In the City

What noise on the summer street rushing with cars and crowded with people under the apartments and church that were tilting over sidewalks and shops, and inside a neighborhood corner grocer's store a loud radio and people choosing apples and cabbages and potatoes from stacked wooden crates and wicker baskets, what noise; and others inside have gathered butter and milk and cheese and sausages and loaves of bread in their arms, candy bars and chips and Cokes, are at the counter, asking and saying things in two or three languages or silent, waiting to pay. Outside on the corner, newspapers are stacked at the feet of a man who goes out into the street to hawk them when the traffic light turns red and for a few moments the poison of the idling engines accumulates. The noisy smell of frying, too, wafts from the restaurants nearby. And past all the cars stopped or rolling slowly, inching forward, whose horns bleat up and down the echoing man-made canyons, here and there amid the roar is hidden the stillness before motion resumes and the stillness after motion has stopped, both stillnesses ceaselessly arriving and dissolving again into noise. It's inside the store, in this man's sudden halting before a cold package of bratwurst or bruised apples; it's outside in that woman's closed eyes while she's standing at the bus stop. And a man on his way through, among all the others this one person whom we know so well, he is closer to us than a brother— he thinks he has just heard his name called out, very clearly, he turns and looks back over his shoulder. He looks across the street, peers into the open doorway of the grocer and into a garage like a neatly organized dry cave and into a dry cleaner, to find who it is amidst this din, if it is anyone, who knows him. The sound glittered like a gem discovered among pebbles in shallow clear water and it caught him abruptly and made him forget what he'd been thinking. But he doesn't hear his name called again, no one looks familiar, he must have heard it in some other name or call, some play of sound that his mind seized mistakenly from the noise to make the similar seem the identical. Did he hear it because without any awareness of his feelings he had wanted to be called, to be summoned? It was his childhood nickname, a name for all of his being that is hidden inside his adult life, not the name anyone now calls him by, it would be a misnaming in anyone's mouth, and he looks here and there and sees no one he might know from back then, no one he recognizes. Maybe it's someone he can't recognize now. Above the streets are a few faces in windows; in this one and that, someone is looking down. The late afternoon's hot and in that window or this someone inside is moving across a darkened room. The call—but this thought can't quite come to him—might have been from the spirit of this day and this place—this smelly intersection—and from the physical resistance of everything that is inert that human hands touch and move, and from the sweetness of those moments of good that some of the crowd will find in this hour. The call to him, from somewhere inside himself, maybe. And above everyone are the roofs with no one on them at all except for one strange creature who might have wings and who seems disappointed; turning back from the edge, where she was standing only an instant before, looking down, her call almost still echoing, and she's about to fly away.

A Man in a Suit

8/27/1992
To: Mr. Tony Szathmari, Mr. Fong Wei

This is the first time Mr. S. has requested
a report from me. I hope that what I am
writing about what happened will answer
the questions he asked me. Please let me
know if there's something else. Two nights
ago, when it was so hot, I was at about
mid-shift and was actually about to go
to one of our two stores in Lakeview but
someone told me I needed to get to our 24-
hour store on N. Clark right away, fast,
because something was happening. What it
turned out to be was that around 1 a.m.,
when it was still very hot, I have learned
from many witnesses, although I did not
see this part of what happened myself,
that this greenish blue raft of ectoplasm
came across the parking lot like a kind of
giant amoeba, nobody saw from where. When
it got near the doors of our big N. Clark
St. 24-hour store, where the light just
pours out of that place, it brightened up
a bit, and people were standing around
pretty fascinated but not wanting it to
get too close to them, and only a few of
them ran off in a fright. This thing kind

of seethed toward the center--it was about the size of a queen mattress--and it slowly lifted up into the air a kind of column of itself, I guess if it was up to me I would say, that turned into this figure of a man wearing a tan poplin suit, white shirt, no tie. I can't say if it was really a man-- his skin neither white nor brown nor black, people could not agree on what it was, he had on very dark sunglasses, his hair was dark and very short. So he floated to the edge of this ectoplasm thing and stepped out of it onto the asphalt like he was stepping out of mud, and he nodded to one man who was standing very nearby--from what that guy told me I didn't understand if it was a friendly greeting exactly, but I figured it was the kind of nod that a man will give to another man just to kind of signal that there is nothing wrong, like a truce between them, no cause for alarm or action, or any feeling whatsoever, for that matter. And then the man in the suit, if like I said it was a man, because when he got closer to the entrance he did trigger the automatic door open, just like anybody else would do, and he went inside. Sounded like a huge number of the seventeen-year cicadas were making a tremendous racket in the trees around the parking lot, too, like kind of an outdoors soundtrack for this.

There are always a fair number of shoppers in our 24-hour store. All types, as everyone knows. Some of the people in the parking lot hung around the ectoplasmic raft and several others followed the man inside and watched him take a cart and go first to the pharmacy section and get some

cold remedy and some chewable vitamin C, and
then in the school-supply section pick up
a couple of ballpoint pens and a legal pad
and a roll of Scotch Magic Tape, and then he
headed into the groceries and bought biscuit
mix, a jar of red raspberry jelly, a pound
of breakfast sausage, a pound of drip-grind
coffee and some no. 6 filters, butter, a half
gallon of orange juice, and a dozen extra-
large brown eggs. I have the receipt for
you, which the man or something did not take
with him.
       People said he did not react to any
other person in the store. Never seemed
to look at anybody. Some said that if you
were standing where he walked by, or you
were near him in the checkout line, there
was nothing different about the smell of
this man. And nobody really panicked or got
weird about this whole thing, which I think
is really odd, like he had some way of not
alarming people even though they saw that
thing in the parking lot.
       The man was a very patient person--he
was at the register of the checkout girl
who only started yesterday. His bill was
$19.92. He paid with regular used-looking
U.S. cash money from his pocket. He asked
for plastic not paper. The bagger handed
him his bag and afterward when he found
out who, or maybe what, his customer had
been, he said that when his fingers happened
to touch the man's, they felt just like
ordinary fingers to him. The man never once
took off his sunglasses. He was trim, about
five-foot-ten, and clean looking.
       Later I talked to some people who had
been standing near that ectoplasmic puddle.

Which kind of quivered and throbbed a little
around the edges and was bubbling slowly
in the center. Even though the man didn't
smell strange, the parking lot thing had
a very peculiar smell, in their opinion.
Something like a combination of burnt
hair and like ozone from off an electric
motor. And it might as well have been a
trained pet, it was waiting so faithfully
for the man, not leaving its spot by the
automatic doors, despite all the attention
being paid to it by people standing around
it watching but staying several feet away
so as not to be touched by it. It didn't
respond to anything anybody said to it,
although several people tried talking to it,
and shouting to it, like it might be able
to hear but not very well. Everybody says
it was only about half a foot thick, but a
little more than that in the middle, where
the man had come out of it. When I got
there later you could hardly hear yourself
out there because of the buzzing cicadas.
When it's the seventeen-year hatch like it
is this year, it's like alien-world sound,
really, and that gave me something to think
about.

Then here came the man or thing like a
man again out through the automatic doors,
people said, and they fell back from him
as he came out carrying his plastic bag of
purchases, wearing that pretty nice suit,
and nicely pressed, too. He was now wearing
a hat, the old-fashioned kind that men wore
in movies--which everyone said was not on
him when he went into the store, or when he
did his shopping, or when he paid for his
groceries. No one else in the store was

even wearing a suit.

He nodded to a few men, the way he had
before, and without looking at any of the
women (one of them screamed, she told me).
And somebody had called the police.

So the man in the poplin suit, not a bit
wrinkled, came real calm to the edge of the
blue-green raft of ectoplasm and stepped
into it and sank right through it and
disappeared into it like it was the surface
of a deep pool and the ectoplasmic stuff
rose in a thick lump of almost a splash
where he had gone through it, and a little
whiff of vapor came off the lump like a
tiny cloud. Several people said that vapor
smelled like a locker room; others were
directly in its path as it drifted a few
yards and they said that it had no smell at
all.

As soon as the man or creature had gone
into the raft of ectoplasm, it gathered
itself in and began to bubble more and
extend its way back into the parking lot,
with people on that side jumping out of its
way as soon as they saw it was coming at
them. Not that many people seemed to really
be afraid of it, which I should explain
didn't surprise me, somehow, although I
can't explain why not. But they sure didn't
want it to touch them. On the spot near
the door where it had been waiting, it left
behind the plastic bag, but it was empty,
although the cash register receipt was still
in it, and that's why I have it now.

Some shoppers trailed after the
ectoplasm. A lot did, and yet nobody ever
said what else it did or what happened to
it, or where it went, that I could find out.

And I interviewed about fourteen or fifteen people about it.

Probably a lot of people will say they were there and saw it, but at most there were about thirty, counting both the parking lot and the store, who did, and a few of them, anyway, were too scared to catch more than a glimpse of it. A DJ from one of the rock stations--the one who says he is going to run for alderman--was on the air this morning about how all this had all been staged by a rival station, but did not say how or what for. The TV Action Eyewitness News van was there but they came too late to get anything on video except the empty spot where the ecto had stayed waiting for its man.

Maybe it was the man that was like a faithful pet of this thing, and it sent him on an errand for it, to bring the fixings for breakfast. Maybe there wasn't any man at all and what people thought was a man was only a remote-control part of itself that the queen-size mattress of ectoplasm sent into our store in that shape so that it could shop like a person and pay for things the way anybody else would.

There was a little bit of a run on the Osco liquor department afterward. No problems, though. Very little additional to add. The whole event has caused a lot of people to do some thinking. I mean, the ones who were there. You've got your green valleys and you've also got your red ones, right? (Along with your dry wadis and your flash-flood arroyos, if you get what I mean.) And you have to think about where you have come to. I mean, it's us that

have to think about it. (I worked on this
report yesterday and I do not mind having to
prepare it and if Mr. S. would like reports
on a regular basis, I would like to do
that.) I need to say that all this is not
just about the man in the suit--you can see
that. How does this kind of thing happen
in this country? I would bet that somebody
in the back office is going to want to make
an ad out of this for the whole chain, but
I think that would be not right--what would
you say? That not just people but something,
we don't know what, also shops with us? One
copy of this report has been sent to Mr. S.
and one to Manager Wei, and I have kept a
copy, and I gave one this morning to a man
who was out in the parking lot when I was
there two nights ago and called me yesterday
to ask about it all, if I knew anything
more, I don't know how he found my number,
and when I told him I was writing it all
up as Mr. S. asked me to, he asked if he
could have a copy and he came and got it
this morning. I hope it was OK to give it
to him. He said he is studying neighborhood
dynamics on Clark St., which I certainly
do think is a good thing. I mean people
need to know about this kind of thing. A
patrol car showed up about two hours after
the incident, and it was not really apparent
to me that they were even interested. I
was still there, talking to people, and I
personally showed them where it happened.

/s/Jerry Wozcik
Group Captain, Night Security

Time Out!

Oh let's say that the great tree that the storm blew down
will be set upright and will grow again. It will!
The wind that pushed it down will stand it up again.
Let's say. You can do it. The storm wasn't that bad, you're
OK. Just put it behind you, that's all.
Who do you blame for your bad luck or your tired
lungs or your sagging life? It's the principle of the thing.
Who are these people, let 'em go somewhere else. For
Christ's sake don't bullshit me. Who's he, anyway, to try
and throw his weight around? Look, all I said was . . .
Fight (sport, spectators, partisans, gambling, money,
hierarchy, dominion, betrayal, bloodlines, bloodshed,
territory, speed, strength, limelight) or flight. Bend or
break, rough it, get moving, pack the heat, bring it on.
Benches, pews, chairs, recliners, bucket seats, stoop
steps. Another used car, tractor, half-ton, coffin.
But didn't get the promotion recently even though
chosen for the parade marshals on the Fourth presti-
gious the management and research team that took it
public then sold on the hobby side of things working
groups Rick has kept up with his life-plan of climbing in every state with good peaks rebuilt his cousin's
cabin when his cousin was sick for a year now they
share it Chief Information Officer proud father of

Sean and Sharon.
Curly organized the union annual laid off when
orders fell carried Mary's piano just with Abe it was
two months then three then four and started spending
most of his time at Louise's fixing up her place cases of
beer we wouldn't even see him funeral was something
hardwood floors overhead blue jeans 12-gauge boots
riding mower a nice bass boat.
Aiee! Buy! CT-scan! Dentures! Gunpowder! Hy-
perconductivity! Urologist! Internal combustion mis-
sionary! Lift-off, prayer breakfast, solar, sell, torque,
wages—the challenge, the network, the commission.
The hernia, ulcer, heart, emphysema, arthritis, bald-
ness, hangovers, back, prostate, hypertension, big C.
Term life, annual interest, Medicare B, liability and
collision, still under warranty, the daughter's games
at school but that boyfriend no never, new whatever
for the wife, the boy's lazy backtalking sad-ass friends,
close-out sale on big flatscreens, consolidated with a
single loan, identity pirates, indoor-outdoor hassles,
minimum wage, job retraining, security system, three
gallons of Kelly Green on sale, I don't trust the cloud,
trigger lock, clogged gutters, rent's overdue, respect's
overdue, discounts on diabetes, what kind of a job is
that, previously owned dentists, fucking Comcast bill,
but did you ever notice how the labels on so many things
at the hardware are so plain and functional, no fancy
wrappers, just saying what it is but then you notice the
hype and you can't trust even trust a screwdriver. What
happened to the genuine male packaging?
To say nothing of 117 to 115, 42 to 27, 3 to zip, two
kings and three fives. All that striving drives the lives
and dries the wives. All the falling prices fail the frail

or hale working man and fill his shoes with lunar-panel crash-and-burn get-and-waste gas-and-*he*lectric yee-haw fuck-you.

Preparations for Winter

Behind our house, across the small yard, the widow's house—the nearer widow's house of the two side by side—seems nearly uninhabited since her husband died. The life inside is so far inside that not even a fingertip touch of it reaches the windows.

Her losses. Her parents, long ago in some other era so remote that the light from it, which now reaches her only in photos, has shifted to yellow. Then this eight-block community that was once an immigrant enclave, a neighborhood of small frame houses and low brick apartments with, then, neighbors going in and out of the small shops for meat, talk, groceries, solace, alliances. (Now the old ones sometimes reappear—from where? Almost spectral they come down the sidewalks once in a while in summer, and ask the young couples up on their porches with their toddlers if they knew so-and-so who used to live in this house, or the one next door, and the new people have never heard of him, never knew of her.) Then the widow's children, who grew up and grew older and grew away—all five of them. Then her husband. While she was out, a thief came in and broke off a leg from a dining-table chair and beat him too hard with it in his living room and took her jewelry.

A year has gone by and now the elm that had filled the sky so hugely with its slow airy striving bulk is gone. I didn't see the long labor of men surrounding it and crawling up into it and cutting it to pieces, so when I came home that day its disappearance seemed instant. Impossible. The small limbs and the sections of the great trunk were gone; heavy sawn sections of the big limbs lay on the ground. Coming through the new openness, cold new light strikes the back of our house. And there wasn't any waiting for the unmanageable great stump of the felled tree to soften and decay. It was chewed up by mechanical force and violently churned into the earth, as if it had committed a crime against men, whose feeling toward it was an enormous obliterating rage.

That was a few weeks ago. In her backyard today two young men are building a wooden crib for the elm wood. A third man is working ineffectually and dangerously at splitting some of it with an axe, having to swing it with foolish vehemence against that stubborn damp wood because he doesn't have a wedge or a maul, probably doesn't even know he should have one or the other. A young man's careless foolhardiness might offer the widow a preoccupation she could make good use of. Even if he's someone she doesn't know, has merely hired, and whom she might fear or distrust. Here he is, enacting his young disregard for his own limbs and life. But she must be inside her house.

And didn't anyone—not either of these men, certainly—tell her that elm won't burn, that it's a mistaken economy or convenience to try to use it in her fireplace, that it's no good for burning and it stinks when it's lit? And worse—if it died of disease, then if she burns it, the smoke can carry the infection to other elms. Who convinced her to have such a solid crib built for the worthless wood of her elm? She's been deceived; cheated; led into error. But perhaps no one needed to talk her into it. Maybe the two men who aren't going to tell her they shouldn't be doing what they're doing are providing her with an unintended gift: the sounds of hammering and a shrill power saw in the still, cold air, the scent of the sawn lumber for the crib, the good wood they're using to build the crib, and then the enduring of the elm wood. The measuring and cutting and making, their flannel work shirts, torn and stained, their jean jackets and their old jeans, their murmured comments to each other, their breaks to have a smoke. The elm logs are dark, wet, rough, very heavy, they're the very lifelessness of the dead tree, still unreduced, still intractable, astonishingly substantial. As if proof had been required by some authority, the tree is now proven dead—its parts will be stacked neatly in the new crib made of other wood, the elm wood will be put into a new shape not that of a tree. Maybe the wood won't even be carried into the house, maybe it won't be mistakenly forced to burn—burn, damn you!—against its own sputtering will, in her fireplace—the very tree that presided over every backyard year of the life of the widow and her husband. Maybe she never intended to burn the elm wood.

I think she needed something new to be done— even if it's needless. Something that's for a future, even a future of not doing rather than doing. We can't bury an elm, so why not make it a memorial presence? A long while to dry out and make its own long slow way back to earth in its own way. After working all day to build the crib and stack the logs in it—only a little of the wood has been split—the men finish the job. The widow's in her house. She'll wait with the wood, there's a sense in which it's not even dead; between the two of them, the wood and the woman, she'll go first, and the dead wood will be her survivor.

Dying with Words

The dirt was bare and the funeral flowers lay twisted and shrunken in the red mud, the gold foil-wrapped cans knocked over, the blossoms all brown. The very day before she died, this woman and her husband had had a fight because she had been worsening fatally for months and he still hadn't bought a plot and she was angry at him for not having bought it. He'd stopped doing anything at all, she'd said. But now she was buried, although there was no stone yet, only the raw mound that had slightly sunk already because it had rained, and the little two-year-old boy started suddenly to dig into it to help her get out.

Someone had told the father that his children must face the reality of death, but no one could explain to the boy, in a way that a child could understand, the why of his mother's going. His father showed him where she had gone—but could not tell him why this was not really where. She herself, like anyone else, had been unable to explain to the very small boy where he had been before he was born. So he couldn't not think that she was under the heap of mud, and he couldn't think that she was, and he began to dig.

No more, for that matter, had she been able to explain to herself how she had "conceived a child," for it had seemed to her that she did think him into existence, lying in bed every night and wishing for him, praying for him, after she had raised his sister for a few years and wanted, needed, a son as well. No more than she could conceive that she was going to die soon.

Lying in her hospital bed between the days when her husband brought her their two children, she had begun to distract herself by looking up words in a paperback dictionary, till this searching was no longer a distraction but a discovery of a string of hints to mysteries. But the answers wouldn't come clear.

She learned to go back farther, she asked her husband to bring her a much bigger dictionary, and he brought it with a resignation that made her secretly furious for a while. She hid her anger from him, just as she tried to hide her panic and fear for herself and for all of them—although he could have borne much more, for after all it wasn't he who was dying. At the same time, she could tell that he thought—because he was not capable of taking the measure of her helplessness and despair, and did not realize that he could not—that his own feelings of bereft loneliness and irritation were stronger, deeper, somehow more important, than her feelings.

She looked up "female," which was what she still was. Her quiet hands were more beautiful than they had ever been; the radiation had killed most of her hair, and even her pubic hair had mostly gone, leaving her looking like a girl. (Yet later, after the big dictionary had grown too heavy for her to hold, she wanted to shave her legs one day, and she had to ask a nurse to do it, and it was the nurse, not she, who cried, bending over the straight, still, silken limbs.) But maybe "female" had nothing to do with beauty anymore. "Female" comes from a Latin word and the Latin word came from other, older, words, farther back from the Romans than the Romans were from her, and it meant "she who suckles," and that is also where the Latin word for daughter, that she liked the lacy sound of, "filia," came from. Or else that oldest word meant simply "to be, to exist, to grow." First we suck, then we grow. Her boy had sucked and grown; she had given suck and was dying. The word didn't apply to her.

Then she looked at "being" and "existing" and she found that in the dark and cold of Norway, whence the word had come to her through ages for her to use without thinking, till now, "to live" meant "to prepare," and it also meant bondage. To live is to be in bondage—she knew someone had said, "Free at last, free at last, thank God Almighty I'm free at last." But she had not listened to him, then. Had not wanted to.

So before she died she thought that after her death she would no longer be female, because she could not suckle her son, and she would be released from the bondage of her illness. There was another word back in that remote eon that made the Romans seem modern, that meant "to retreat with awe," and she began to do this, backing into her own death, awed not by the death that was coming but by the life she was losing. *Don't leave*, she said to the three of them one afternoon, by which she meant that she was leaving.

Her husband, to whom she had been bound, and her daughter, whom she had raised for a few years, and her son, whom only months ago she had fed at her full, unaccountably painful breast, went to visit her grave. (It had been dug only six days before, by the same discreet laborers who, one day later, had stayed away from the burial, behind large headstones, and then, keeping their distance, had approached at the backs of the mourners returning to their cars.) Carrying in his mind an idea, some bad advice, a witlessness, her husband brought the children back to see the grave, days after that. Rain had fallen during the night. He himself was not wondering where "she" was; he was putting all that out of his mind so that he could live through this day. He had so wrapped himself in his own arms, for comfort, that he was excusably, perhaps, far from his children and the things, every little one of them, that had excited or pleased or pained *her*, all the daily sensation and stuff she had clung to more tightly as she had sickened. They were very different persons, he and she—they had been.

The little girl felt that her mother would hide from her forever and never tell her what happened, what was happening. Although she felt that what the grave held might not be a person, she was angry. Then the boy put his hands in the mud and started to dig, getting filthy, thinking maybe of her beautiful breast, the one that had been left, and wanting a voice, a warmth, and all else that was gone.

Her husband had wanted to make love to her in the hospital. That came at something "female" that was not what she had tried to understand. She hadn't let him do it. He had chafed at his own grief and new responsibilities; another sort of man, in his place, might have cried and kissed her. But she lay dying and turned her head away from him to spare him the judgment she knew was in her own eyes, and to take her eyes off the further injury he had become to her, in his simple ordinary failure. She was sorry she had had to reach the end of her life to learn that a terrible trial or terrible need would not bring, as a right, some saving presence, a rescue, a mothering. This man, this woman. How it went, with them. Among all the unnamed and unnameable things is not only what the little boy wanted, for which no word is large enough; and the undeniable longing his father felt in the white hospital room empty of the true noise of life; but also the sort of kindness, finally, that the wife gave her unwitting husband when she turned her face away from him so he would not see what she felt, when she let it go, let it all go. We can dig through all the dictionaries there are, we can muddy our arms to the elbows with words, and we won't find the word for that.

On Belmont

"Watch it, brother," he said. He who had come up beside me without my even noticing him as I was walking on lively, crowded Belmont one summer night. He dropped into a squat, half-leaning against a building, a brown-bagged bottle in one hand. "Get down," he warned me.

Ragged, stoned, looking full of fear. I stopped near him.

I don't think I had heard even a backfire.

"Machine guns," he said. "I know, I was *there*," he said, turning his head from side to side.

"Not machine guns," I said—to be helpful. Then I had what I thought was a good idea. I said, "And even if it is, they're a long way from here." (They'd *have* to be, suppose it *was* possible, they were still blocks away from here, at least, off down the busy late-hours streets lit too bright. We had plenty of time.)

"Oh," he said, meaning, Is that what you think? With a quick glance. His gaze sidelong, and strong. It would take too long to teach me. But he explained: "That's when they're really bad, that's when they get you, when they're far away."

He stayed low, one knee half up, squatting on the other thigh, protecting the bottle held half behind him. He looked up and down the street. I waited as long as I could, maybe half a minute, but all this was over now, that was about as far as we could take it, now that we had had our moment of contact in this world, after our separate years of wandering other streets and other countries. We had happened to be momentarily side by side at the sound of whatever it had been, maybe a gun. I started on down Belmont, I got back my pace, I was heading for the train.

Maybe to him, still squatting and leaning there, not yet ready to stand up, or able, it seemed like he was the one who would get to where things made sense and were safe, and I was walking foolishly in a place of danger. How could he explain it to me, it was way too late for me and everybody like me.

Mission

After she had been in her kindergarten for months already, one afternoon at home she was crying because of something a friend had done or maybe only said to her, and I was trying to offer some solace, some distraction, when she nearly shouted all of a sudden, "You and Mommy left without even saying goodbye to me!"

I said—shocked to have caused a wound so lingering that other pain must inevitably lead back to it—"When?"

"The first day of school!" she said, and she really began to wail, looking up at the ceiling, tears pouring from her, her face crumpling.

"But you wanted us to leave—you were lined up with the other kids to go into class behind the teacher, I thought you were happy to go in!"

"But other parents were still there! And you left without even saying goodbye!" The way rain can arrive with a violent flurry of pouring and thunder but then settles into a steady fall that is the real rain, that will after a while flood gutters and basements and streets and fields and rivers till there's damage it will take time to repair—so she settled wearily and deeply into her crying.

However a wound was caused, it is there, it can't be undone, it needs to be healed.

This child is standing before me on the carpeted stairs down to the back door, her eyes level with mine as I sit on a higher step holding her hands, and she is crying as if she will never stop, and the friend's slight is forgotten, the first day of kindergarten is forgotten, there is deeper sorrow than that, incomprehensible, and for now I am feeling the longing and protective presentiment that bind me to her in love, and I understand what I must do as long as she and I live, and how much I want to do this—love her—and need to do it, and that it is not enough. It is the way of things, and no blame on anyone for it, that it won't be enough.

Just Imagine

Long ago, if you'd gone to the window where my first lipstick left a mouth on the glass that I wiped off with toilet paper, and you looked out at an angle as sharp as you could get, putting your cheek to the cold glass that was so dirty on the outside, you could have seen that, just as anybody but Mama would think, there was nothing out there on the other side of the fifth-story wall of our living room except the wind that blew around the tall apartment buildings day and night. I'd kissed the cold window, like saying a prayer please let there be something more for us (like she says sometimes). But I knew there couldn't be. Mama was convinced some-times—not all the time—that if only we could secretly break through the living-room wall, the same wall where the photograph of her mother had been hanging for so long, then we could find another room that nobody knew about. That no one but us would be able to use. A room just for us—Mama, Donald, Desmond, Bobo, and me. "I'm telling you! Go look out the window on that side and you'll see it," she would say hoarsely to me sometimes. She said it like it would be my fault if I didn't see it waiting for us. And even if I had seen it . . . we still couldn't have gotten into it. I used to think— if only we lived on Orchard Street, wherever that was, such a nice name for a street.

Mama almost never went out, so we had to get everything for her, when we got ourselves organized and the money was there. In the living room, the bedroom, and the kitchen, which was the whole apartment, there would often be Aunt Jean, Mama's younger sister who was a loud visitor, but she brought us special things to eat, Mama's friend Zulie, who was a quiet one and too bad she helped us eat them, and Bobo, yapping. And when Desmond was a baby, on some weekends it seemed like he cried about the same number of hours that working people worked. Donald was always a quiet boy. Mama herself almost whispered instead of talking, so you had to get close to her to hear her, which was what she wanted. And me. But I'm not criticizing them. I wish I could go back there, I wish I could just come through a door from the imaginary room and say, I've got a big hot meal waiting for you that I made myself! And see them all crowding in like Christmas.

The secret room had a deep green carpet. And a little piano. And a big lamp with a decorated shade that made a soft yellow light, and a big red easy chair just for reading. It had pictures on the wall. It had lots of windows but the room was never cold. And the city looked different through them. Lights in those office buildings and skyscraper apartments to the east were kind of cheerful and cozy instead of far-off and lonesome—they said come over this way for a while, even though I had never been over that way, never been to where the mountain-buildings were. The secret room had a wooden bookcase painted a pretty green with books in it. And it was quiet in there. Oh, you could still hear the talking and noise from the living room and the kitchen and the bedroom, but muffled by that shut door. You could have laid down on the clean carpet and stretched yourself out any way you wanted and slept, it was that clean. No Bobo piss. No dust and dirt. And nobody stepping on you when they went by. Nobody shouting or yapping.

Donald is seven years older than me, nine older than Desmond. Donald went to California and stayed there. I don't know him, really. Desmond had me to look after him and he did OK—he drives for UPS. Mama was smart, she was determined, and if she had had some opportunities, if she had gotten more schooling, she might have been president of a company instead of turning into a woman who was not completely in touch with reality. Especially not in touch with it after she raised kids and only had a husband for a few years. I'd look in my head for something I could actually say to her and then I'd say it, so she wouldn't think I was sulking. So I grew up quiet, like Desmond. He and I. But my not saying much could make Mama angrier. Poor Mama. Nothing went right for her.

The roofs of our building and the three others like ours were flat. The last staircase, leading up from where the elevator stopped on the twelfth floor, was made of metal and was steep and ended at a door that opened onto the roof. No one was supposed to go there. That door was supposed to be locked, but the lock was always being broken. For a while somebody tried to put a big chain and padlock on it, but people knew how to break that, too. The roof was dried tar or something, so if you walked on it, the soles of your bare feet in summer not only got way too hot but also got dirty. And your shoes too, any time of the year. Inside the twelfth-floor hallway there were always black tracks on the floor. And just like on the ground around the building, there was junk up there, too—bottles and cans, some old wood or metal things, busted up, lying here and there. It had a low wall around the edge. But something was beautiful about being up there in good weather. You had to be careful though not to go there when the wrong people might be there already, or might come up on you.

The clouds moved, the sun moved. You couldn't see but slivers of the lake far away, here and there, and some larger sweeps of it where all the buildings weren't in the way. But at night the lake made this clean edge and giant place of complete dark *nothing*, out past the whole lit-up city and especially the mountain-buildings. Hard to describe the feeling of looking at that—it was like everything, everything, ended at the edge of the lake and there wasn't anything else there, no water, no ground, not even any air, nothing. Donald slept on a cot he put up every night in the kitchen, Mama and Bobo slept on the couch in the living room, and Desmond and I slept in the little bedroom, and then when Donald left, the cot disappeared except when somebody outside the family needed someplace to sleep, and Desmond moved to the couch and Mama and I slept in the bedroom, with Bobo. We figured most things out. We lived with it.

I would find the right spot up on the roof and get down on my knees at the edge above where our apartment was, I'd hold tight onto that little wall, and look over, straight down the side of the building and count the floors down to the fifth, and I could sort of see where Mama's secret room would have been, sticking out from the side of the building, if it had been there. I so wanted to believe in it even though I never really did, even when I was maybe four years old.

I'd feel sorry for Mama and ashamed of myself for wanting her to stop saying the room was there. To stop believing in it. On hot summer days and nights, with all the windows open, we would gasp for cool air that might have been in the secret room but wasn't in ours.

And time did pass. I graduated from high school, went out on my own and worked a day job and took classes at night, gave money to Mama, and I did well, I was always good in school, I just tuned everything else out, and then I got my MPH in another night program, it took years, and I ended up . . . in one of the smaller mountain-buildings, in my own little place, with my beige sofa, my good table and chairs, my red easy chair, my pale green bookcase, my Chinese rug. I can look out my windows, facing only west, not toward the lake—right over the city, toward where I grew up. I haven't been out there for fifteen years. Desmond comes to see me, brings his two daughters to see their aunt. His wife is very different from him and me, but we all get along. Under the fading sky after I've watched the sun go down far away beyond the endless streets, I imagine all of us, back then—the way, back then, I imagined the secret room that I actually come home to now. (Except I don't have a piano.) The only one of us I find, when I get here, is me. When I think of Mama holding Bobo, and of Zulie and Jean, and Desmond and Donald, and me too, once upon a time, and some cousin or friend of Mama's on the cot at night sometimes, all of us getting on each other's nerves but just doing what people do—working, living day by day

in that old way, birthday parties with mostly just us,
and wishing for more, maybe imagining, and willing
to give something, for some room they can't see and
can't find that would make life so much better, sometimes I feel like—

Small Business

Into the ground-floor, storefront office, past the three staff—the secretary ("Hello, boys, he's in his office—"), the accounting clerk (who is always annoyed at anything like this), and the assistant manager (who doesn't even notice them)—to the manager, come the two twelve-year-old boys.

The manager is rumpled, bent over his desk, scribbling something on a pad.

"Hi, Dad, can you give us some money to go to McDonald's?"

"Hey—two hungry men at large, alert all kitchens." (Without looking up from his desk.)

Then he does look up and adds, "Why? Don't you have any money?"

"No—we want to go to McDonald's."

"It's four o'clock, you're going to be late for your game. Did you take the bus here?"

"No, we're not."

"Don't you have to be there by five?"

"It's not till five-thirty."

"Oh. Did you take the bus here?"

"So can we have some money?"

"Don't you have any left?"

"We were going to go to the bank, Keith was going

to get some out of the bank, but it was closed."

"Keith—you have a bank account?" (The manager is surprised, curious.)

"Yeah. A savings account." (He is, in fact, holding a little blue book.)

"Oh." (To his son:) "Am I picking you up at home? You have to get your game stuff, right?" (He's still holding his pen.)

"Yeah. But McDonald's?"

"You have money at home, right? I'm only loaning. How much have you got at home? When you go to McDonald's with friends, it's on your allowance, right?"

"At home I've got eight dollars."

"OK, here." (He counts out bills from his wallet.) "Take these eight, and now you owe me your eight. How did you get here?"

"Well, Mom owes me five, so you could just get the five from her, and I could give you three at home."

"She owes you five?"

"Yeah. Could you just give me ten? You have a ten?"

"What does she owe you five for?"

"Because she didn't have all my allowance on Saturday, and she still hasn't given it to me."

"That's not the way I remember it—I thought she was holding back five dollars for the comics you weren't supposed to buy."

"No—I don't have to pay her back for that, she said. Didn't she tell you?"

"No."

"She said that was OK, because after I finish reading it again I'm going to give it to Brian. He's in the hospital with a broken leg. He broke it really bad."

"OK, but if you have eight dollars at home, you

already owe them to me, because remember I'm still waiting to get back the twenty dollars I gave you so you could pay for the jersey to replace the one you lost at school, and you spent it on something else instead. That kind of thing—"

"That was on school supplies—remember, Dad? And you told me that was OK."

"—is important—to be responsible for your money, right?"

"You told me it was OK."

"I did?"

"Well, could we have ten dollars, Dad?

"So if I give you ten now, how much do you owe me?"

"Will I owe you something?"

"Yes, of course you will!—you'll owe me the ten bucks, I'm only loaning it to you, like I said."

"Yeah, but that was before we talked about the school supplies. You don't remember stuff sometimes, Dad, like the twenty for school supplies."

"No, I think I would remember that."

"Please? You're going to get the ten dollars right back! Mom's going to give you the five she owes me, and Keith's going to pay me back tomorrow for his half."

"Look, just take the eight dollars and we'll talk about it when I get home. You have a little more time than I thought, but you make sure you get yourself home and get your stuff together, and be ready to leave by ten after five, Mom and Dougie are picking me up, then I'm dropping them off at his peewee soccer practice, so I'm just stopping the car in front and honking the horn, and we're going straight there, OK? OK?"

"OK."

The boy grins winningly at his father, who smiles back at him with instantly helpless love and exasperation, and then he looks at the papers on his desk, to remind himself what he had stopped working on. Keith has not said a word. But he whispers to the manager's son as the two boys turn to go out, and the manager's son stops and asks, almost over his shoulder, "Are we ever going to get the car radio fixed?"

The manager does not look up from his papers. He says, "I don't know—get one for your bike."

"Yeah."

The two boys grin at each other and go out the manager's door and past the assistant manager, the accounting clerk, and the secretary, who at her desk that's too small for her piles of work, is balancing a checkbook she's holding in her lap. She doesn't notice the boys at all, and they don't notice her. The manager calls after them, "Hey! How did you get here? Did you take the bus?"

On Assignment

The little boy whom I'd last seen about two hours earlier, the one wearing a tattered T-shirt and raggedy
jeans, came up the dirt road carrying on his back a
huge load of long sharp-edged leaves that had been
tied in a bundle with lengths of vine. He was maybe
seven or eight. Bent over. Holding the vine-ends with
both hands at the back of his neck, his little dirty elbows sticking out in front of him. In a tree overhead a
bright red and green bird was whistling its ideas about
everything. A kind-faced priest wearing only snake-
skins, sneakers, and a skirt of feathers blessed the boy
as he went by, and then took another sip of his Pepsi.
At the top of the slope, a shiny Hummer with a flatbed
trailer hitched to it was waiting, and it seemed like this
boy's bundle was the last that was needed, because one
of the three soldiers there—who were wearing work
gloves, while the boy had none—took the bundle from
him and threw it onto the load, and the three of them
got into the Hummer and drove off, spewing mud and
gravel behind them. The boy came back down the slope,
standing up straight now. I was ashamed and stepped
out from where I'd been hiding. The look in his eyes
was wary—fully as much of me as of the soldiers. It was
early afternoon, and he had to be hungrier than I was.

Everything around us was growing fast in the hot wet narco weather, and inevitably he would have to grow, too. The priest never said much. Who knew what he was thinking? I'd learned he wasn't allowed to show up back at his strange kind of group house till dusk, or they would punish him. Clean water hadn't been reinvented yet. I was writing everything down on white lotus blossoms and floating them away on the muddy stream nearby, and keeping a mental photocopy for myself. I was making something like a tiny model story of the real story, I was making believe, making do, making up what I could never make up for.

Dead Man's Things

Well, change from a dead man's pockets, for instance—a quarter would be a powerful frightening object to have in your hand when we were kids if it came from the pocket of a dead man, like that guy shot by police whose change spilled onto the sidewalk when he fell, that time.

Somehow these coins were more powerful than the money of a man of no power who wasn't dead yet, but only dying, like that Nigerian student who came to Chicago and sold ice cream from a truck in the summer evenings and who was shot in the neighborhood and people called 911 and waited and waited till the police and an ambulance came after a while and he had bled out onto the sidewalk while some kids darted up now and then to take ice cream and money from his little truck.

You had a dead man's hat for a while, bought at a garage sale for two dollars, a beautiful gray Stetson with a rattlesnake-skin band. He hadn't been wearing it when he was killed in a car crash, and his brother didn't want to keep it.

You have some things of a dead man who was your kin—your uncle—and whom you loved because of what he was and what he had done even though you only saw him a few times in your life. An old small Persian rug, that he had bought in 1930-something from a stranger who'd come to his door and asked your uncle if he'd give him five dollars for it, which he did. That man too, dead now too, certainly.

You have only one thing from your uncle's father—your grandfather—which is the way you used to set the knights on the chessboard, facing not ahead toward the coming battle in which they are likely to perish but at their queen and king, like he taught you when you were little.

You've got some clothes of one dead man—a few things given to you by his son, pretty worn out now. You didn't know him well but you admired him. When you put that red wool shirt of his on, you sometimes think of him and thank him for helping you onward after he stopped coming with the rest of us. And other clothes—even a coat, the most sacred of all clothing, given to you by the widow of another man, a friend who was another uncle to you and whom you loved.

Of your other grandfather maybe you have the way you put out your hand when you say certain things, or maybe even the way you say them, who knows, you'll never know, he died when you were two.

And from the man whose coat you used to wear only once in a while in winter, and that later you gave to someone else who loved him, too, you have the greatest thing—the words you speak if you read aloud from his books. And the shape of your breath and the beating of your heart as you read, and the space you're inside when you're in his work and away from everything else, or maybe his books take you *into* everything else; and you marvel at what he had and wonder where did he get that? Did dead men or women give him that? Which ones? Or who did he take it from, darting up near him as that writer lay bleeding out in one way or another from his body or his body of work before the police came to arrest him for having bled or readers standing around him turned their backs and said nothing? Did he grab a coin he took from a dying writer's books and shove it in his pocket till it was his time to spend it?

Slow Motion

Once, quite a while ago, there was this guy at one of the pay phones, saying: "Yes, sweetie, what do you feel about that? Were you scared of the way Mommy was talking?" Everybody could hear his voice all over that corner of the hotel lobby. When you work with a system, you can get angry, but on the other hand you don't have to make any effort at compassion—which is beside the point. If it isn't doing its job, it's not because something bad happened to it and it has to take care of its feelings, or you do. The guy's voice was tender. But I could hear his resignation—he couldn't change whatever was going on at the other end of the line. He said, "I'm going to be home the day after tomorrow, do you think you can get yourself ready for bed tonight, and then get up and go to school tomorrow, because then I'll be home the next day, OK?" Some systems are stupid, some smart. If it's down, that's even better, that can be a gift to me from the company, not my problem, I'm not the one who fixes them. The man was saying, "Mommy is very tired, and she needs to be alone for a while, can you get ready for bed by yourself?" His cigarette—he pulled on it deep enough to suck the smoke all the way down into his legs. Then while he was stubbing it out in one of the hotel ashtrays he said, "I know you don't want to, but you can do it, you're a big girl now." Even back in those days, the room reservations for the next hundred years were in the system, along with credit card numbers, phone numbers, addresses, company names, titles, and all kinds of stuff that nowadays has all been stolen from us, probably. Security, or doing the job, running a batch of updates for the next day, back then, if you knew what to do, was a piece of cake. No point being anxious about it. The guy looked at his watch, it was almost eleven p.m. where he and I were, he crumpled his empty pack and tossed it at the trash can and missed. So the kid had to be out west in Pacific Time. He was listening a long time. The only other person at the desk with me—I'll call her Heather—was poking along. People come in, they want a room and have no reservation, they received one room and now they've had a fight and want two, or they went up to their room, put the key in the door and opened it and there's someone else in there. You know. I had this problem with Heather—I still have it with everybody. "What *did* you want to eat for dinner? Did you want a peanut butter sandwich like I make for you?" He started fishing around in his briefcase and he found another pack of cigarettes. He whacked it on the counter a few times and tore it open with both hands while he held the phone in the crook of his neck, and he tapped the first few a little bit out of the pack and took one with his teeth and lit it with a match from the hotel matchbook lying on the counter beside the ashtray. Then he held the phone to his other ear. My problem especially with Heather but with everybody, and I can't help this, this is just the way I am, I don't do any drugs or anything, is that I'm always waiting on them to catch up to me. Just catch the fuck up. Back then you used to call information for a phone number and you'd sit waiting while this recorded voice says the numbers one at a time starting with the area code, so slow I could write it down six times while she says it once: everything else is in like slow motion for me, everything but me: I'm in real time and everyone else is going really really slow. OK—we don't wait on the phone for phone numbers any more. But the faster things go, the faster we need them to go. The guy tucked the phone into his neck again as he got out of his suit coat one arm at a time—put the phone on the other side, held it with hunched shoulder, and folded the coat and laid it over his briefcase, which was standing on the floor, and all this while he's listening. Then he said, "Yes, honey, I know you felt bad, I know you were worried, but you don't have to worry, Daddy doesn't want you to worry, everything is OK, you can go to sleep and have happy dreams, and then go to school tomorrow, and Daddy will be home the next day." He lit another cig. I would run a routine on that system while I was showing Heather—jeez, I still remember that too-sweet smell of her shampoo—or somebody else how to do it and they just wouldn't get it, and I'm supposed to show them how to do it so that I don't have to be the one to do it, I'm supposed to be supervising, troubleshooting, not doing the daily runs. But for me it ends up being easier just to do it—faster, I mean, a lot faster, than it would be for me to go over it again with somebody new, and instead of doing the right thing I do the thing I just feel I can't not do. "Honey?" the man said, "You need to go to bed now, sweetie, it's time to go to bed—where's Mommy now?" He looked pretty sad. My mother was crazy, and that's no lie—she had to be as crazy as that guy's wife. When I was eight years old she went for *months* of that year without speaking to anyone in the family. She pulled back so far from me, my sister, who's older than me, and my father, and my father's sister that lived on the next block over, that we almost got used to her that way, and we would talk about her when she was standing right beside us because since she wasn't saying anything to anyone it was like she had gone away somewhere, like not only did she not speak to us, but we didn't see her. The guy said, "I'm going to send you a big kiss through the telephone, OK, just like I always do?" He stubbed out his cigarette, listening, and exhaled a cloud of smoke, slow. "I'm going to send you a kiss, are you ready?" I remember the cigs especially, since I was still wanting them so bad myself, at that time. He smoked four, I think, while he was on that call. She didn't even talk on the phone to other people, and we were having to say, week after week, that she couldn't come to the phone or was out or was asleep. You can want something you can't or shouldn't have and it's just up to you—OK. It's so much worse, if people would only understand, when what you want isn't up to you. She came back to us, that time, when I picked up the phone one time just before dinner and it was her old boss and I went ahead and asked her, like we always did, while I covered the phone with the palm of my hand—my father taught me to do that—did she want to talk to him? She surprised me and came and took the phone—he had called to offer her her job back, after she'd been home more than a year because the strain had been too much for her as he'd been losing business because of his own screw-ups. She was a good secretary and he realized he wanted her back, he was doing better, he was willing to have her, crazy and all. And I was amazed to be hearing her voice again—I had forgotten it, almost, forgotten what it was like when she did talk. I actually liked to hear her voice, I waited and waited for it, she had a beautiful voice, but there was something in it that I never got, that she never gave to me, and maybe she didn't give it to anyone, certainly not that I ever heard, but I thought I could tell it was hiding inside her, not coming out all the way, when I heard her talk the way she did that night to her old boss. "Here it comes!" said the man on the phone, "Here comes the kiss, are you ready?" He listened for a few seconds and he said again, "Are you ready?" I really couldn't concentrate. I can remember that whole conversation he had. I couldn't do what I was supposed to do, and Heather was down the counter from me totally lost in something or other she was probably botching on the other terminal, I didn't know and didn't care. In those days I really didn't. He said, "Here it comes!" and he made a loud kissing sound with his lips. "Did you get it?" he said. He had a huge smile on his face to make his voice sound cheerful to her, and it did sound cheerful, but she must have been crying, and he didn't say anything but just held the phone to his ear for a while, listening to her, or maybe listening to the dial tone because she had hung up or had the phone hung up for her or who knows, but his face wasn't smiling anymore. I've seen photos of me when I didn't know I was being photographed, and I've got a very not-smiling face. This guy's not-smiling face was also his usual face, I decided, except when he could blank all of this out and pretend to be enjoying his time with the business people he had to joke with to make a sale, or when he could get several drinks in him, or both. I bailed out and set the system back to ready, and this was weird—I remember for some reason that my arms felt so heavy. That whole scene I was watching had done something to me. Once in a while just like that something goes wrong, like you know there has to be a reason for feeling physically something's wrong that's not physical, but you can't get to where you'd know what that's about. I can't, anyway. I saw the inside of some hospitals in my time, including mental—back when the day rooms with everyone in pajamas reeked of cigarettes and their hair was all goofus and the loud TVs—jeez I *worked* in a hospital once. "Data processing," then. Where I never had to interact with a patient. Some of the administrators, too, in fact, were more or less batshit. The guy hung up. He puts his elbows on that old narrow marble pay-telephone-plus-ashtray counter, I'm talking about a while ago, no pay phones now, no ashtrays, and he puts his face in his hands. What did he care what other people saw. End of episode. Another one coming soon enough, no doubt. He was feeling it. I was feeling jumpy, feeling like everybody else was in slow-mo. I like the late shifts, but I had hours to kill, and—although I have an excellent memory for just about everything, a really unusual memory that is not in every way a blessing, let me tell you, and although I can still see that guy, can still hear those long pauses when he was just waiting, when he couldn't do anything about it all—I do have a good memory, it's almost like those people who remember everything, but at least it's lucky for me that it's not really that, and there's nothing else about that night after he hung up that I remember.

Persephonē at Home

No spices—only salt—and no ice or coolness. The food
she has to prepare is dry, stale, gray. The pantry holds
mealy flour, dried beans, stale crackers, and hard dried
figs that taste of must and sweat. Holes in the dining
room floor, big enough for her foot but where she'd
better not step, open downward into a deep bottom-
lessness, absolutely dark. There even Pluto doesn't go.
And in his kitchen sink a stink rises when upstairs any
water runs.

No room without a little smoke in it; and beyond
the window curtains there's only black emptiness outside, through which the less tormented shades come
near the house, floating slowly or sometimes hurtling
past, eternal strangers to each other but whispering or
moaning to be heard, anyway. So she keeps the curtains
closed while she's there; she can scarcely bear to touch
them when each year she must move back in, they are
so filthy with accumulated smoke and dust and vapor
of burning oil.

The darkness is hot and humid, and in it he works
all day, she never asks at what. He doesn't bathe often
and until she can get used to this again she tries to
hold her own sleeve—clean at first—over her mouth
and nose when she greets him. In bed she must cover

her face with the bedclothes in order to fall asleep. The sheets are gray despite all the washings she gives them, and black soot spots the gray. The water she must use for washing and cooking is gray. The air seems gray.

Her days—sometimes she merely stares at a small candle flame for hours. She must overhear, without wanting to, the sounds from outside the house, where she doesn't venture: there is no full voice among all the shades, no resonance of sound in their world, and in it something is clicking randomly all the time. Pluto himself, although not a shade at all but godly in his way, with his huge beautiful physique and the exaggerated features of his face, like those of a statue meant to be seen from far below, has an odd voice—not big and also a little high. Repeatedly she washes out her clothes. There is never quite enough light to sew or even cook by, but she must do it anyway. She awaits the passage of days and weeks and months in a realm where each dim hot hour seems a day in itself. Then he comes in suddenly—there are no warning footfalls in a landscape of dusty paths and mists.

His frustration—although, to describe him, "frustration" suggests too much delicacy—is that it's not within his power to inflict any torment great enough on those outside the house to make them go away, and that it's not meant for him to change his rule to the world above. He believes that he loves her, and when she's away he pines—although, to describe him, "pines" suggests too much feeling. But he cannot rescue her from the conditions of her life with him, which have been set by divine powers of tradition and the generations of gods. He cannot change the half-year of nights when she cries to herself in a wing chair in a dim corner, without a window she would want to look out of. In a way, he is almost happier, or at least less troubled, when she is gone and he can only think about her, during the half-year when she is above again and happy and he is still below, at work ruling and being, without need of rest or change.

When they are together in bed, sometimes she can remember her excitement at his first attentions to her, although these had been rough and he had come to her in that other world, her world of air and promises; she thought she believed that she needed something of him. But when she decided to refuse him, and her mother agreed that she must, he carried her away by force to keep what he said was already his. Together in the hot darkness—in his house, in the season when she is with him—in bed what they do is mechanical and efficient and quick for each of them.

Then she gets up and goes to the front room, away from him, and sits in that corner of hers in that chair, which he has joked at her about—her little throne!—and she falls asleep there.

She does not try to explain to him how she can read his every impulse and thought so easily; he doesn't realize she is far wiser than he. The darkness of his realm is in part ordained and in part is his concealment of his own nature from himself.

All the shades are estranged from themselves, he no less than they, even though he's not at all a shade. Unlike them, he can feel hope—because *she* must always return. That's the holy custom. Yet if, in his once-in-a-while tender moments, he would ponder her needs, he cannot see them. Even if he could give her what she wants, he cannot accept why she keeps wanting what she wants.

It embitters her to know that, in the world above, despite all her life-giving beauty, things were not so different. She was sweet and strong, and her effortless power of germination and blossoming—which she had used then as she uses it now, when she's there, not here—no one there except her mother had noticed. Not till they lost it for half the year. Or asked themselves what she wanted or felt. Except flowers themselves, she thought, and orchards in fruit, and the golden wild barley. (They asked.) It seemed to her now that no one then had cared a fig about her.

The fig is an oblong or pear-shaped fruit, pulpy when ripe, and eaten raw or preserved or dried with sugar. Green, red, purple, soft, moist, fresh, cool, sweet.

Courthouse

Once upon a time / there was a little man / who ate little children.
>He had a wife that ate children, too.
>Once a little kid came and got ate up!
>"Gee, I've eaten a lot of kids!"
>They made a gate with the bones.
>And the bones got bigger and bigger.
>Some of the bones was so big that *nobody* jumped over them.
>Only the person that made the bones, and it was God.
>He made the bones littler and littler.
>The man that ate little children, he died.
>The woman died, too.
>The end.

Your honor, testimony of this sort proves absolutely nothing at all.

Over and over the little boy drew a snowman. A three-year-old's unsteady hand holding a colored pencil. Then the hand was four years old. The little boy said, "It has hair in its mouth, it has hair in its mouth." He stopped saying it after a year, and drew the snowman wordlessly. The teacher's aid had been arrested and let go. Then arrested again. But when the boy was drawing the snowman, when he was saying, "It has hair in its mouth," nobody understood. He was not trying to tell them something. He was telling them something. Why didn't they say they understood?

~

Where you wait to be called, first they screen a junior-high-school-level TV slide show recapping a false history of America from revolutionary days to the present, showing cartoons of the judicial branch and finally photos of the modern courthouse, and there's exuberant rock-and-roll music as background to the loud voice-over. *YOU: THE JUROR*, says a male military voice. *NINETY PERCENT OF ALL JURY TRIALS IN THE WORLD TAKE PLACE IN AMERICA. THESE ARE THE PEOPLE WHO WORK IN THE COURTROOM, WHO YOU WILL SEE: THE JUDGE, THE CLERK, THE COURT REPORTER, THE ATTORNEYS AND LITIGANTS (THE PROSECUTOR SITS NEAREST THE JURY—WITH THE PLAINTIFFS IN A CIVIL CASE), THE WITNESSES, AND YOU, THE JUROR.*

PAY CLOSE ATTENTION TO EACH WITNESS WHO TESTIFIES, DO NOT MAKE ANY INVESTIGATIONS OF YOUR OWN INTO THE CASE, THE OPENING STATEMENTS AND FINAL STATEMENTS ARE NOT EVIDENCE, THE JUDGE WILL INSTRUCT YOU CONCERNING RELEVANT POINTS OF THE LAW.

There will be peremptory dismissal and dismissal for cause, there will be the swearing of the jury, and the jury deliberations, and the verdict, and the Battle Hymn of the Republic, and . . . *A CITIZEN, AN HONORABLE MAN OR WOMAN, A JUROR!*

～

From the Dan Ryan Expressway and the TriState Tollway, from suburbs and all three sides of the lakeside city, into all the courthouses come hundreds of judges. Should they arrive drawn by steeds in carriages with livery? Should trumpets sound? They park their Accords and Navigators, their Cherokees and alphanumerical car models and they set the alarms. In the jury pool waiting room, on the three color TVs, loud game shows and celebrities and then, as the jurors wait, the soap operas come on—people blackmailing each other, abusing each other, killing each other, hating and tormenting and hitting each other with their words or their fists, coloring each other various shades of green and purple, modeling their product-placement clothes, they're shouting and intravenous and wretched and relaxed and good-looking and low-calorie and crying. Waiting, the citizens in the jury pool watch, don't watch.

～

A little hand points, not very precisely, at a person sitting behind a table.

～

"I'm making allowances, Judge, as I know you must be, for the fact that the witness is very young. But in fact, Judge, the pointing was very inconclusive, even though my client was *looking* right *at* the witness!"

～

The other day, when I asked you to tell me a story, and you told me about a man who ate children up, was that really about someone you know?

No.

Why did you draw the snowman?

I didn't draw a snowman.

⌒

THANK YOU FOR SERVING!

⌒

Home again, home again, jiggety jig.

Winter Friday

After I shovel the snow and come back inside, something more needs to be done—like dragging a big black plastic sack through the upstairs rooms, emptying into it each wastebasket, the trash of three lives for a week or so. I am careful and slow about it, so that this little chore will banish the big ones, for now. But I leave the bag lying on the floor and I go into my daughter's bedroom, into the north morning light from her windows, and while this minute she is at school counting or spelling a first useful word I sit down on her unmade bed and I look out the windows at nothing for a while—the unmoving buildings, houses, and a church, on my white and black block.

Across the street a young man is coming slowly down the white sidewalk with a snow shovel over his shoulder. He's wearing only a light coat, there's a plastic showercap under his navy-blue knit hat, and at a house where the sidewalk hasn't been cleared he climbs the steps and rings the doorbell and stands waiting, squinting sideways at the wind. Then he says a few words I can't hear to the storm door that doesn't open, and he nods his head with the farewell that is a habit he wears as a disguise, and he goes back down the steps and on to the next house. All of this in pantomime, the way I witness it through windows closed against winter and the faint sounds of winter.

My daughter's cross-eyed piggy bank is also staring out the window blankly, and in its belly are four dollar bills that came one at a time from her grandmother and which tomorrow she will pull out of the corked mouth-hole. (It's not like the piggy banks you have to fill before you empty them because to empty them you have to smash them.) Tomorrow she will buy a piece of impeccably small furniture for her warm well-lit dollhouse where no one is troubled in any way and the wind can't get in.

Sitting on her bed, looking out, I didn't see the lame and odd neighbor child, bundled up and not in school and even turned out of the house for a while sometimes, or the blind woman with burn scars or the sick veteran—people who might have walked past stoop-shouldered with what's happened or keeps happening to them. So much limping is not from physical pain—the pain is gone now, but the leg's still crooked. The piggy bank and I see only the able young man whose straight back nobody needs.

When he is finally past where I can see him, it feels like a kind of music has stopped, and it's more completely quiet than it was, an emptiness more than a stillness, and I get up from the rumpled bed and smooth the covers, slowly and carefully, and take a wadded dollar bill from my pocket and put it into the pig and walk out.

Harlequin

About two weeks after Bill died, while I was sleeping I saw that I was at dinner in a restaurant with others. Bill too was at the table. He was dead; but alive again except that his eyes remained tightly closed, and he looked bad. He was animated, he talked a lot, with anger and happiness, and the others seemed amused, and not a person remarked on his coming back. He was dead, though, and his body showed signs of his decaying. The skin of his face was leathery, blotched, peeling. It was a horror, but no one seemed to think his being there was horrible. I tried to understand.

The next night, he came again—again we were eating at the restaurant. But Bill showed further damage, his skin yellow and stained and his hair reddish and long and dirty, and he talked with even more energy, dominating the conversation (as he hadn't done when he was alive), and the others again only amused, no one horrified except me. Maybe they don't see that he's dead? But I know.

In the second restaurant scene something happened, I've forgotten what it could have been, and Bill, holding his eyes shut very tight, began to talk faster and faster (about what, the dream wouldn't let me remember), and then in that sudden instantaneous way of dreams we were somewhere else, and Bill turned into other things. Persons, I think. It wasn't Bill at all. Was it a spirit of which he was an inextinguishable part—and of which others are parts, of which everything is a part? Is everything? In waking life, I don't believe this.

This spirit into which he changed was transformed by a power beyond Bill's own through a hundred shapes in a hundred seconds. (But were they forms of animals or persons or things or beings never known or seen?) We were outside, on a high pleasant grassy slope, with prospects and vistas. When the changes stopped, a kind of tall youthful harlequin was standing where Bill had been—gaily dressed, laughing.

The harlequin, holding his audience—I alone—bent down to pick up from the perfect grass a tiny sequin of a jewel. Perhaps I was the first to see it glittering in the grass and I asked him what it was. He comes nearer and bends and picks it up. I don't touch it because it's so bright, it's blue-white, I can't look straight at it, it hurts my eyes. The harlequin picks it up between thumb and forefinger, and smiling he tosses it into the air with a snap of his wrist, upward. It rises, it soars on a long curve up into the sky, growing larger and even brighter and it becomes the sun.

Near the Spring Branch

Sometimes I wish the way I see things had not changed
so many times and I could still hold to an earlier way
that didn't need something huge to open me up to
the thrilling airiness inside that later I would get only
when I was where I could see, I could feel, something
big—a mountain summit; a canyon under a storm where
there might come a roaring flash flood, and I do mean
flash; the night sky over the open sea; a huge reading
room in a library; a mass grave; a military parade with
tanks that shook streets and sidewalks all down the
avenues; a whole city abandoned and then ruined by
the centuries and by later people who scavenged its
stone; a lonely kid who talked to me in a huge empty
city square because I was a foreigner and he couldn't
tell anyone he knew what he wanted to tell.

To recover that early, that first, way of seeing, even
for a moment, would require working back in memory and trying to forget my first sight of a mountain-
ous horizon, from a Greyhound bus going west from
Dallas into New Mexico, summer I was seventeen. To
get back before that, so I could feel it again for the
first time. I'd have to rid myself of the Pacific Ocean,
with Poseidon under it, and of that completely different creature, the Atlantic, to which someone first led

me by the hand, pulling me into its tragic waves; of scabby-ankled men on hot city streets; of off-duty Marines beating up some peacenik families in Houston and nobody stopping them, during that war we lost, and I had no way of stopping them; of the sound of whites talking about blacks, and talking to blacks; of a monstrous pyramidal slave-labor brick kiln I saw in a far country, lost as I was on some small remote road that led closer to it till I could see what it was and I kept going so I could get away from thinking about the man-ants climbing the sides of it with wet-new-molded mud bricks on their backs and tumplines across their foreheads; of the summer view from a high hilltop church of a saint, at dusk when distant village lights began to burn and blink like earthly stars in the valley below; of a tavern high and alone amidst the trembling intense green of rainy hills, and men sitting and drinking at tables outside, and in a cage that was tied by a wire to a pole near the tavern wall, a fox; of all the other mind-images I have formed and sights I've been formed by, that come back and I can't see the connection between where I am, what I'm doing, who I'm with, and whatever it was in a particular moment that suddenly opens up inside me one of these intensities and I'm there again for an instant and then it's gone again.

I would also have to forget the little commercial enterprises and small houses modeled on inappropriate but perhaps forgivable grandiosities that came to crowd our road like warts along the vein of a smooth, plain, dark hand. Everyone out there was building a house. And just with my mind I would have to restore a field of the ordinary weeds and bushes and bare patches of white sandy-dusty earth of an old eco-zone where some company gradually dug a huge straight-sided quarry hole finally sixty feet deep and hauled sand and gravel out of it, and then abandoned it, a pit so huge on our little scale that to us, standing with awe and a thrill of fear on the edge of it where our parents had told us, begged us, sworn us, never to go, it suggested a cataclysm. When the diggers hit clay and stopped and abandoned that hole, by a year later it had half filled with half-clear greenish water in which nothing ever lived but algae, and finally we had to think of it as some kind of lake in a hole, and somebody fenced it around and posted it against trespassing because new houses rose closer and closer to it and finally someone's child drowned in it.

I have to go back before all of that and before so much else, to the moment when our own house was the last one on that road, in a place with only a few trees, and I can remember some birds—doves of three different kinds, one time a quail, some bobwhite, meadowlarks, mockingbirds, redbirds . . . The rain would stop. Killdeer tracks—as delicate after they ran across the rain-wetted bare ground as if some hand had carefully drawn them in the fine pale prehistoric silty sand—ran across the open ground between clumps of pale bunchgrass and yaupon bushes till the hot sun dried everything out again and the sand-silt-dust drifted softly over itself.

I saw a photograph taken more than a century ago—a man in a suit lying on his side and up on one elbow at the only unusual spot in a flat empty landscape looking like where I grew up, but in his day when it was miles and miles from one stand of trees to another, from one house to the next: this unusual spot was a small concavity, a shallow sinkhole grown over with short-stemmed weeds, maybe twenty feet across and not more than four feet deep at the center. Was this the grand natural curiosity of his locale? He's posing on the other side of it for the camera, and the edges of the photo imply the empty expanse around him, and so maybe he has a greater sense of how odd and noteworthy his sinkhole is. He brings the photographer with him all the way out from town to take his picture—in his trousers and jacket and white shirt, lying with his head propped on his hand, and the photographer makes a trophy for him of his admiration of that depressed ground . . . or his mocking of it . . .

I want to show you the fresh track of the killdeer. On an afternoon of a coolish breeze in hot summer, after a green and black thunderstorm, the torrents of run-off might have filled the ditch beside our house and come up over the banks into the front yard so you couldn't tell any more where the bank was, the ten-foot drop. The next day the ditch would be down to a depth of five feet, and still flowing so fast that it could easily carry you away and under. The slightly cooled air seemed to have been created anew and not yet used for anything. Once in a while in summer, after a gentler rain, our mother would hand us each a plastic bowl and say go across to the field and pick some plump dewberries and I'll make a cobbler for dinner. And when you come back take your shoes off outside and don't track mud into this house! The four of us crossed the ditch on the two-lane wooden bridge that was still there, then, before it was demolished and replaced by a wider concrete one with railings, and on it the name of somebody.

I would need to forget that new bridge to get back to what I'm trying to see, and yet I'd need to remember, too, that after big rains like that it was wonderful to lie belly-down on the wooden bridge with your legs sticking out into the lane—we would hear a car coming in time to jump up and get off the bridge—and hang your head over the edge and watch the drowning murky flood go dizzying by, floating leaves and twigs and trash and sometimes a snake. I'd have to forget that many years later I would learn that the deep ravine, a streambed, around Mycenae was called Chaos.

Across the bridge we entered the empty field on the left side of the road by slipping through the half-slack barbed-wire fence, and always we cast a glance over at the ten or twelve good big trees over in the field on the right side of the road, a grove, so powerful a presence of trees and even (in our child minds) of some kind of little gods, a place so strange in the wide emptiness, a mysterious place that we sometimes visited together just to feel what it was like to stand in it. The shade itself, the cool soil under the fallen leaves, somehow different from every other place we knew. But we never *thought* this feeling. Over there, too, we would find the temporarily engraved tracks of the killdeer, a bird that runs across the ground piping loudly and then flies away. In the flat bare sun-bleached spaces between yaupon bushes and between clumps of bunchgrass, tiny tracks in the shallow slicks of earlier rain. And in the berry field closer to home, tiny tracks near the low mounds of tangled stickerbushes of wild dewberries heavy and freshened by the rain.

As we tramped, those killdeer tracks were to us as much a hushing proof of wildlife as the sight of a lion would have been to someone else somewhere else—and years later and farther west, walking on a hilltop at the edge of a western city, looking down at the streets and houses and big buildings downtown, I came across the prints of a cougar in mud. The killdeer flew through my mind again, calling *dee-duh-duh-dee*. Picking berries gave us tiny blood scratches on our hands and wrists. We might see a horny toad, or some kind of snake, *stay out of its way*! The breeze would finally begin to blow hot again and bugs would come up into it. We could pick a couple quarts of berries in a short time and Mother would cook them down in her quick crumbly dough.

I'd like to have stayed behind, though, just once, till the others were through the fence and hurrying back over the wooden bridge to our house, and I think I might have lain down on my side next to an open patch of sandy silt with my white plastic bowl of dewberries, next to the killdeer's pronged footprints and then I'd have told my photographer to open the shutter on me there. I could look at it now, but I still wouldn't see as I saw then.

Change the Goddamn Thing

The reality of it. It lay on the table, neatly organized in a neat pile. So many pages. There it was, lying there. And he circled it and circled it steadily, loopingly, picking up this or that desk toy, fiddling with it, rearranging something else, looking at one thing or then walking straight into the next room to get another, stepping cautiously and circuitously the way a tiger might circle a staked goat under a tree in whose branches waits an unjustified and irrational rajah with a loaded rifle across his lap, or the way a hyena circles a lion that's feeding on the carcass of a narrative idea.

His beech tree with runes of his carving scored in its bark. His book.

It is his increase, his verbal incorporation, his augment, his augury, his auxiliation; of which he is, or will be considered to be, or will be suspected of being, or will be suspected of not being, the author.

It is his mud, his lap, his slobber and slaver, his label on all collapse and all completion, his labor, his very lip, his life's work.

He must prosecute it yet further, he must sequester himself with its intrinsics (and extrinsics), he must designate and assign it sufficiently and properly, then when he has finished he must dissociate himself from it and throw it to others. Inside the jet-engine howling of market mechanisms and the anti-aphrodisiac of book reviews, where something or nothing will be made of it, it will be hefted and had, havened or captured, perceived, righted and wronged, received or chased away.

Can it be, friends, that he was confused where the road forked, and forked again? Or did a gale shove him off course? What power could help him find his way? Had he himself created the fork, blown the winds at himself, disempowered himself, because something deeper in him knew better where to go? But the rest of him did not seem to know.

So there it lay, awaiting the attention he has not been able to give it, the focus it does not quite have, the final touches he may not be able to add, the feeling-tone it has failed to establish, the box in which it will not fit, the protagonist it has not fully animated, the progress it has sketched but not made forceful, the postage that may be insufficient. Near it and much bigger lay a messy pile of unused bits, crossed-out pages, notes on characters, outlines, diagrams, quotations, scrawled questions (some of them angry-looking, written in caps and followed with multiple question marks), etymologies, diagnoses, etiologies, case histories, transcriptions, confiscations, spoils, search warrants, wiretaps, recipes, photographs, genealogies, philosophies, cosmogonies, theodicies, peripeteias, maps, lists, this piece called "Change the Goddamn Thing."

It lay there. He circled around it. He growled. The pendulum of his beloved old clock swung back and forth quietly like a heavy twig broken by wind

and dangling by a strap of its own fibers. The sky outside sometimes whirred. He kicked up the leaves on
the floor of his study, he tested the blade of his knife
against his thumb.

What Happened

Sally left town because her family back home needed
her to help get both grandfathers into nursing homes.
Geoffrey was angry because he thought a letter meant
for him had been stolen by Dean, but Dean could prove
he was out of town when the letter was supposed to have
come. Geoffrey wouldn't say what was in the letter, and
pleaded with Dean to loan him two thousand dollars
as soon as possible. Preacher Jim asked Samantha to
go out to dinner with him, but she refused, saying it
wouldn't be at all fair to Margery. Mr. Talltower began
negotiations to acquire the luxury Fountain Hotel, but
Melissa accused him of avoiding her and the children,
and even the grandchildren. On a very hot evening at
the beginning of July a young man left his little room
at the top of a house in Carpenter Lane, went out into
the street, and, as though unable to make up his mind,
walked slowly in the direction of Kokushkin Bridge.
Young Preacher Jim, still in his twenties, tried for the
world preaching endurance record but had to quit at
a little more than thirty-two hours when the tip of his
tongue split in two and began to bleed and he couldn't
drink any more hot coffee because of the pain. Everyone had always said that Jim would be a preacher
when he grew up, just like his father. Margery insisted

he go into the hospital for a few days of rest (thinking he might dry out). In the hospital he saw Frank, who had a new job there as orderly, and he preached to him for an hour. Samantha's custody suit was set back when Cal's lawyer won another delay. Frank stole drugs from the hospital dispensary for Geoffrey. Dean heard on Newsradio 88 that a prairie fire was slowing traffic on the outbound Nixon Expressway, and that on the outbound Lincoln Highway it was taking an hour and twenty-six minutes from Downtown Exchange to Forest Mall. Traffic was still slow where the volcano had erupted last week and poured molten lava on the road, and also a meteorite had blasted a crater near the Brewery exit. Lynnette was unhappy. Dusk—of a summer night: in her backyard, her fig tree was filled with fruit. Cal was offered a job by Mr. Talltower, but turned it down because he didn't want to earn money he would just have to split with Samantha. At the shelter where Margery does volunteer work, over a hundred homeless people, counting children, went out of control and mobbed the volunteer staff for more heat and blankets. Dean realized that Geoffrey was scheming against him and he vowed to get even. Gisell had to miss little Clark's play because of her migraines. The schoolmaster was leaving the village, and everybody seemed sorry. Strange creatures from outer space landed in Preacher Jim's big backyard and promised him the secret of eternal life if he would come back with them in their spacecraft forever. He asked them for forty-eight hours to think it over. Frank told Geoffrey that Dean was onto them. Mr. Talltower decided not to buy the Fountain Hotel but to try to buy a male country-western singer instead, because Melissa loves those songs so much. When Dean heard this he said that there are some things that are so much just what they are that you can't even make fun of them because you could never think of a way to carry them any further than they've already gone, and that Willie Nelson had more money in the bank than a beach has sand. In a house near Lynnette's, a family was trying to raise their children to be loving and responsible, to work hard and demand an honest recompense, to hold, all their lives, ideals of compassion and fairness, to remain skeptical toward all politicians, to be brave and to give no quarter in struggle, to do what is right. Overnight an orchard grew in a street on the east side of town. The Martianness—she went out at five, or came back, nobody was really sure. That very night Mr. Talltower's son arrived home directly from the war, where he had personally killed three people and had himself been killed twice. He walked into a party Melissa was giving but everyone was so shocked to see him they didn't know what to say. Finally Melissa said he should get married, have children, keep his powder dry, stick to a low-carb diet, take one aspirin every other day, and get counseling. He went outside. A throng of bearded men in sad-colored garments and gray steeple-crowned hats, intermixed with women, some wearing hoods, and others bareheaded, was assembled in front of a wooden edifice, the door of which was heavily timbered with oak, and studded with iron spikes. Lynnette was unhappy all that night and the next day, too. Preacher Jim saw Samantha in the Village Ice Creame Shoppe and asked her if she would go to outer space with him. She said no and he felt very frustrated.

There were floods and tornadoes, and fire drills at the schools. Problems of folklore are acquiring more and more importance nowadays. Preacher Jim, who was so upset at losing his chance at eternal life with Samantha, said signs of the end of the world are everywhere and that as soon as he had his strength back he guaranteed he would break the world preaching endurance record. Frank decided to have a mind-change operation in Denmark, and the only person he told was Lynnette, who said he shouldn't do it because something like that was against the will of God. The patrician house of the Marcii at Rome produced many men of distinction. Mr. Talltower decided he would buy the Fountain Hotel and have Willie Nelson sing in it. Geoffrey voluntarily went into a detox center. Samantha and Dean decided to get married as soon as her divorce from Cal came through. Jill returned from a trip to Central America, where she had gone to a libertarian resort, modeled for a video game TV ad, and had been given all the cocaine and purchase options she wanted. A train carrying radioactive waste with a half-life of 10,000 years derailed behind the Community Swimminge Poole. A whirling ball of flame descended onto Main Street for five minutes and then turned into a bright yellow Coke machine. No one had ever seen anything like that machine, which had a built-in TV and sold Cuba libres, too. It was revealed that a famous literary scholar who had died had written Nazi journalism when he was young. Mr. Talltower's son re-enlisted and left town. Frank went to Denmark. Dean saw on TV where all kinds of wars were going on in the world. Cal and Samantha had one last bitter argument in front of everyone. Several flights of imagination came to rest on the Towne Ponde and everyone went to see them but they flew off and didn't come back. The strike at the Meate-Packinge Plante went into its sixteenth week but nobody knew anyone who actually worked for it except Mr. Talltower's daughter who was on the Board of Directors, and she said that she had been assured by the plant manager that despite the strike the company was able to keep the hormone and antibiotic levels of the meat as high as they had been before. Cal kidnapped his and Samantha's little Patricia and disappeared with her. It was about eleven o'clock in the morning, mid-October, with the sun not shining and a look of hard wet rain in the clearness of the foothills. The movement of tectonic plates went unnoticed in the town. Some writers have so confounded society with government as to leave little or no distinction between them. Winds swept out of the west and cleared the smog for a day or two. The moon swerved suddenly farther away from the earth and the tides went crazy and there were reports of flooded cities. There was a choir out in the orchard. The average world temperature went up another degree and there was new desert in Illinois. Sally came back from helping her two grandfathers.

A *Singular Accomplishment*

Laz Hart used to be able to put his toe in his mouth when he was standing up, could still do that when he was a man, and used to make everybody laugh thataway. He's eighty-or-so now, he preached Daddy's funeral sermon, thirty or forty years ago—didn't you know that? And when we were near the Old House one late afternoon with Jim in his pickup poking along we drove by a place where a skinny white-haired man was out front puttering at the aluminum rowboat he'd somehow put up on the roof of his big beat-up station wagon, although it didn't seem like much of a day for fishing, with the weather blowing in dark and fast. It was Laz, and Jim stopped and called out to him, and he came to the driver-side window. He nodded and said hello and kidded Jim about being back in the neighborhood, where long-ago cutthroats and renegades remain a favorite local legend, especially among those whose lives have been lawful and mostly mild, albeit sinful, too, for as many as eighty years or more.

The matter of Laz's old antics came up—his putting his toe in his mouth. Abruptly he stepped back a few paces, his baggy overalls flapping around his bony age in the green gusty wind before rain, and he reached down to his huge laced boots and as he straightened up he pulled his right foot all the way to his face and put the toe of his boot to his teeth, grimacing with a big smile, and when we stared at him in great surprise and couldn't think of what to say, he let go of the foot and stood on it again and backed away with bashful pride. As if he, the retired preacher, had just invented the very wheel of human civilization but wished not to take too much credit for it.

Three Persons on a Crow

It's flying behind a gull that is flying behind an osprey that has a heavy fish in its talons. Below is a silvery blue river. Somewhere above, there might be a thieving eagle that none of them has yet seen, on its way down in a swooping dive to startle the osprey into dropping the fish and escaping, and then the eagle will catch the fish before it falls back into the river from which the osprey took it.

On the crow's tail sits a very tiny boy, last in order of authority but happy with the wildest ride, holding stiff feathers planing this way and that as the crow steadies itself in the gusts behind the gull and behind the osprey ahead of the gull. The boy whoops and yells in his very small high voice.

The boy's father is riding as if on a horse, sitting on the crow's shoulders with his legs dangling down in front of the beating wings. He's clutching black feathers tightly with both hands, trying to look brave.

The mother, vulnerable and endangered yet somehow with an air of worthiness and sufficient will, is standing straight up on the crow's head! She doesn't need anything at all to hang onto, she's looking ahead at the erratic gull and beyond the gull at the strong great-winged osprey clutching the fish, this is a procession the great consequence of which only she knows, and if the crow would fly ahead much faster why she'd leap onto the back of the osprey, eagle be damned, and ride it into a genuine myth.

Hide and Seek

And the youngest child, out of an unnoticed sadness, would sometimes go into the utility room when no one was looking and crawl behind the green curtain over the wooden cupboard without a door, she would put herself with the dirty shoes and odd tools and other things that were only used once in a while. She would wait for someone to notice her absence, to notice that she was gone, to notice—and then to come looking for her, full of need and worry for her. She was waiting for someone to want to find her: Where'd she go? Where is she? Let's find her! Because: we can't go on without her. Because: we love her. Because: we need her here, with us, now. Because: We love her more than anyone!

But the other children did not come. They kept on playing, they weren't going to come, so after a long while she would have to crawl out again; she always did, from this place she had chosen near Daddy's old shoes—now his work shoes for around the yard. Mother hadn't liked looking at them; she was the one who, from the shelf above, had hung the heavy green curtain. Daddy's ugly shoes.

Now these many years later I'm looking into every room of the house of our lives, looking for you this year and last and always, and just now I have thought of the green curtain which time has hung over all that, to hide work's hard long days. I'm going to creep quietly toward the utility room and step down the little half step from the kitchen onto the cold linoleum floor and find you! I'll call out, Here she is! I found her! I'll carry you on my shoulders to the living room where everyone is waiting . . . Daddy's gone. Mother's gone. You're not behind her curtain. You're not his old shoes! You're the heart of what we have always wanted, and wanted to live for—and we stop everything to find our missing one—without whom we can't go on: you.

Arms

In Chicago, on the dusty floor of the single shop window of a neighborhood used-vinyl-and-CD store where teenagers not so far beyond childhood hang out, the owner has put a discarded department-store mannequin, or rather the upper two thirds of one. He's put a summer nightgown on her that's thin and lacy, the length of which lies rumpled around her cut-off hips as though the hem has risen on water that she has stepped into—thinking of doing what? On the surface of the same pool some old album covers are floating around her.

Appropriately, her head is bowed, her eyes cast downward, you can't see her face because draped over her head is a large piece of delicate white fabric like an oversize bridal veil—a parody of a veil? I don't know how to tell—and it hangs down as far as her breasts and a little lower. And also she has no arms.

A sort of half-clothed, unintended allusion to the statue called the Venus de Milo—to the idea of a woman with no arms or legs? But that connection, rather than investing the mannequin with some added ironic significance . . . that connection between this mannequin and the ancient salvaged figure throws some light in another direction. The mute dummy shows what it is that the Venus de Milo herself represents for us in her broken state, disfigured in a way that has for so long, and even cozily, fit the psyches of acquirers and connoisseurs and maybe all of us.

I hope there's some use in my saying the rest of this.

There's the attraction of the beautiful powerless body. Powerless when represented without arms; powerless when it is the small body of one who, without having lost arms or legs, is small.

I only want to say what seems to me to be there, in the intuitions we share. A day doesn't pass when the experts aren't writing books and pamphlets and explaining yet again to juries about little crayon drawings of children, drawn by children, in the aftermath of the things I mean, which you can figure out—and so often the children draw themselves without arms.

The Oldest Man in North America

It came back to me the other day as I was walking up the Lakeview Road again—very slow for me nowadays, but it's paved now—and wishing I could still talk with you. You and I were up there, almost exactly a hundred years ago, that day we realized we were beginning to feel something for each other. The same time of year as now—late summer. We walked up all the way to the intersection with the Highview Road, talking. Looked around from up there and then came back. We stopped under all those big trees at the front of Carson's property—only two of them left now—and were talking. We noticed there was some new sound—a steady noise of a kind we couldn't even be sure we heard, couldn't be sure we didn't hear.

Over in Albert's woods, a quarter mile from us, he was shooting his shotgun again and again—we couldn't imagine why or at what, but knew who it was. There were a lot of things we were used to hearing. Orioles and wrens and warblers in the orchards. Men calling to each other, yelling sometimes, and horses, and the horse-drawn machinery, during harvest. In spring I had to help Dad in those years by plowing the narrow side field with the mule. It was hard if a young man hardly even weighed enough to keep the plow deep in the soil—it makes a quiet noise, you know, slicing, hissing, through the dirt and clinking or scraping on stones. In the weeds there was all that clicking, rustling, buzzing in summer. I'm thinking of those numberless flying grasshoppers that take to the air just in front of you with every step, in late summer. Trilling, whistling, braying, mooing, snorting. In spring and fall, there would be sandhill cranes in V's so low their honking would echo off a big barn. There was sometimes the sound of crying or a scream, of course. Fussing and weeping, as well as laughing and giggling. Our feet crunching the gravel all the way up there and back. It was a beautiful long walk, wasn't it. Whispering of poplars and cottonwoods when there was a breeze, as there was, I'm pretty sure, on that day that I'm remembering now, one of the early times when you and I did that. Remember hearing that raven fly right overhead, the soft whipping of those wingtips. At a perfect moment when the autumn air and sunlight could make the world, or at least our little part of it, stand still, do you remember what it was like to hear the sound of one single falling leaf as it hit the ground? It was noisy when the wind was up, the trees swaying, and nearer the water, the sound of the lake waves, the moored fishing boats making the hawsers groan. Don't all these sounds put you in mind of others you have heard? But as you know, what we heard that day was none of these.

To say nothing of all those sounds you can't hear, but you know that something or other sure can hear—the fluttering of those little yellow butterflies that will congregate over a patch of mud in late summer. (They were there again, the other day; not nearly as many, but for now they're still in this world.) By the side of the road, the sound of the growing of the wild carrot. The sound of the beating of the heart of a kingbird perched at the top of an apple tree, when it's just about to leap up and take a tiny bug from midair. Sound of stone stories lying in the ditches and heaped up in crude fences, that almost no one ever hears when they crack in winter. The sound of the black trunks of the orchard holding up the wet branches. That deepest sound of all—of the wide blue horizon when you've climbed up high enough to see a lot of it, as you can from the crest of the Highview Road. It's a complex quietness I'm talking about, that's filled with all kinds of different silences.

I was thinking of you again, today. How I do think of you. There was a noise we heard, first time ever on that day, that got louder over the years, and later we were sure we did hear it that day, and after a while we couldn't not hear it, and then we couldn't hear much of anything else. I wonder if you'd have remembered it the way I do. We saw the new century come sputtering and grinding to the top of the rise, carrying some visitors, to get a nice view of what had just become the past.

The Living

A typical hearing or trial in juvenile court, on the delinquency not the abuse-and-neglect side, is like a routine brief dance. The public defenders work from a table to one side of the small plain courtroom, facing the raised bench, the state's attorneys from a table at the other side, also facing the bench. The clerk calls the next case. An official leaves the closed courtroom by the doors at the back to the waiting area and, holding them open, calls out the minor respondent's name. Through another door to one side of the bench, the minor respondent himself—a handcuffed boy—is brought in by a uniformed officer, and the boy and guard stand just inside that door, waiting. The boy is wearing street clothes. A long moment later—"Someone is approaching, Judge," says a public defender, to placate the impatient man behind the bench—into the courtroom from the waiting area come three women. The judge says, "Is mother here?" "Yes, Judge," says the public defender, and he indicates one of the women. "And who is with mother?" the judge asks. "Grandmother and aunt," says the public defender. The judge says, "Aunt, please sit at the back of the courtroom," and the woman retreats without speaking. The other two wait where they stand, also silent.

Like the women who are here for him, this child is black. Except for him and his kin, everyone else in the courtroom is white. The boy's handcuffs have been removed by the officer, and, as instructed by this man, who accompanies him and stands behind him, the boy comes into the courtroom and faces the judge, keeping his hands behind him as if they were still cuffed, and holding in his hands a light jacket, a tube of toothpaste and a toothbrush.

This legal episode lasts three minutes. Approaching the judge from her table with a manila folder in her hand, the state's attorney speaks; the judge speaks; the public defender, standing beside the boy, speaks; the person of whom they all speak is not asked to speak and does not speak. Although they have had time, in their service, to learn a little of the language that the boy speaks, they do not speak a language that is in turn intelligible to him.

Some interim step having been taken, to be concluded later, the boy is led out of the courtroom through that door at the back, the three women who have witnessed the hearing but have not been allowed to touch the boy or speak with him, leave together, talking about a Christmas present for him, and the clerk calls the next case. There are a lot of cases to be heard before the day is over, and the judge wants to deal with each one as quickly as possible.

The boy's public defender gathers his papers, whispers for a minute to one of his colleagues about another matter, while the next very short hearing or trial begins—whether to be delayed again for one reason or another, or concluded—and then the boy's public defender goes out the same door through which the officer took the boy.

~

That door leads to a corridor. Along it are the chambers of seven or eight judges. At the end of the corridor is a raised police desk. To one side of this, where five or six officers stand on duty, talking loudly among themselves, is the "holding tank," a single large room with a glass wall facing the police desk. In it, about fifty boys aged sixteen or younger are waiting— standing, talking, yelling, sitting, remaining silent, looking out through the smudged glass wall and glass door, and being watched by one or two of the officers.

Nearby, the public defender meets with his client in a small bare windowless interview room. The client is fourteen years old and has been held for two weeks, so far, on a very serious charge. His hearing, which will take place in two more weeks, will determine whether he will be tried as a juvenile in this building and have the chance to go free again, after seven years of detention, or will be sent to the court at 26th Street to be tried as an adult.

This boy is short, thin; he does not look directly at the public defender—his attorney. This man is explaining to him what happened in the courtroom in those three minutes of the judge's time. It was decided that something will be decided. But this explanation, too, is in the language of the courts. So in response to the explanation, which is that he is going to be given psychological tests, and that he needs to be completely honest with the doctor, and then there will be another few minutes before the judge, to determine where he will be tried, he says, "How long am I going to be in here?" For his crime, if he is convicted as an adult, he would be likely to remain in prison for most of the rest of his life, or all of it if his life is not long.

His attorney says, "That depends. But it's gonna be a while. We have to convince the judge not to send you to 26th Street, right?"

"Right."

"You know how we do that?"

"Oh man." His knees are jiggling.

"You know how we do that? You have to do two things—you have to not get written up for anything while you're here, and you have to do well in school, upstairs. Are you doing well in school here?"

The child is not doing well. And he has already been written up once. People get in his face, he says. He says he has a temper. All he really wants to know is how long he will be in here.

"It could be a long time," his attorney says.

"*How* long? Am I going to get out for Christmas?"

"No."

"No?!" He doesn't believe this man is his attorney. He says he wants a *good* lawyer, he wants to pay five hundred dollars and have a *good* lawyer.

He shifts in his chair, again and again. The small brick-walled room doesn't fit him any better than his clothes. His jacket, toothbrush, and toothpaste lie on the table.

Even in here, coming faintly from beyond some corner or from behind one of these bricks, there are voices which—whether they're endangered or dangerous—are still free, on the street, still loud out there. That's the world he knows. He doesn't know any of all the other worlds. He and his friends are wary of those other worlds.

"Is it more important to you," the attorney says, "to react when someone is on you, so they *know* you won't tolerate that, or to spend the rest of your life in jail?" The boy says nothing.

"If the judge hears that you got written up, he's gonna think that you're not taking this seriously, and if that's what he thinks, then he'll decide that you need to go to 26th Street. Right?"

The attorney has never studied the development of children, but he has talked with hundreds of them in their hard moments; he is only—out of his own good intentions and his legal training and seven years of work in the institution of justice that is reserved for juveniles—their defender; he despairs of succeeding in more than a small number of cases in defending them adequately and as they deserve; he persists, however. The child fidgets violently in his chair and flings his arms to one side and then the other. He looks at every corner of the very small room and not at his attorney.

His attorney says, "Someone gets in your face, you have to walk away from it, right? And in school, you need A's and B's. OK? That's so we can ask one of your teachers to come down to the courtroom and *tell* the judge that you should *not* be tried at 26th Street. Right?"

From the meeting rooms, the judicial chambers, the police desk, the holding tank, the unconcluded child is returned to a part of the building that is behind additional locks. After he is gone, the attorney, standing in the hallway, sees the mildly questioning look on the face of another public defender nearby. "He isn't going to make it," the child's attorney says. "What he has to do in there is more than any adult could be reasonably expected to be able to do. And he's only fourteen. I couldn't have done it at fourteen." "Could you even do it now?" asks the other attorney. The day proceeds. More trials, more hearings. The courthouse empties out. All the different worlds, here and everywhere around here, go into the early dark of the winter day. After rush hour, whether at the street corners where things happen and traffic goes steadily by, slowly, or at the safe corners where nothing should occur, the snow falling since the hour when the judge got up from his bench and left is making everything a little quieter. Lights and lamps and TVs, through the apartment and house windows of this neighborhood, throw a soft inadequate brightness into the streets. The avenue and streets intersecting near the front of the great building—its courtrooms, detention center cells, schoolrooms, offices, its bleak cafeteria for workers and visitors, the big foyer with metal detectors, the multistory garage—these thoroughfares lie in the strange, nighttime snow-light of streetlamps and headlights. There's some quiet.

And inside the holding tank, there's no one. And in the dining hall of the juvenile detention center, there's no one. In the cells, it's noisy. Boy children and some precocious men who are very young (and a few of the small number of girls and girl women) are in each other's faces. Taunting. Pushing. Threatening. Threatened, pushed, taunted. Outside the dirty unbreakable windows, tall city buildings to the east are like rigid galaxies of costly light. Light snow is falling faintly through the abyss between here and there.

All-Out Effort

I have cleaned off the old radio and put new batteries in it. I have brought my old boots up from the basement and cleaned and polished them. I have brought the old rocker down from the attic and repaired the arm that was broken. I have washed and dried and ironed the old khaki pants and the old soft long-sleeved green shirt that have been hanging for so long at the back of the closet.

In the quiet time before the working day is going to end, out the kitchen door and on the back landing in the afternoon shade, three floors above the trash cans filled with this week's garbage, I've put the rocker, I've set the radio down beside it and turned it on softly to the right music, I'm wearing the khakis and shirt and boots, I have sat down in the neighborhood.

To prepare myself, I brought back to mind one time when from a sidewalk at night we could see through windows the lights and motion of a brightly lit room crowded with people and no one could see us: that moment. I've recalled sitting at my desk in the attic and writing you a letter and the summer sweat dripping off me onto the paper.

I've brought back to mind the words I said to you at different times, and I've spoken them again to myself, wearing these same clothes that I wore in those days. I've begun to return to so many places where we breathed and lived and passed through. Often I have had lots of ideas and I started off with many thoughts, but not one of them was able to reach the end it might have headed for, or even a resting place on the way, or find what I wanted to discover that I felt I was after. Everything that was over was too far away. Even though I chose a summer day for this, or it chose me, I know this green shirt may not be warm enough when I'm crossing frozen fields and cold streets and shore hills of ice, or cool enough when I'm back in hot nights buzzing outside with cicadas and tree frogs, sirens and shouts and engines and shooting. Where I'm going, there will be hot sweaty rooms with shallow-breathing windows, there will be hurricane waters, cold winds will whistle through the cracks in me.

Like a long-legged river bird, I was wading but now I'm flying, I'm off, I'm headed back into places not of now, I can hardly hear the radio voices, a little wind of time is starting to whip my trouser legs and my sleeves and make my eyes smart. Let the tears come! This rocker is getting up some speed. I'm going back, I'm going to rescue at least a little of it!

Acknowledgments

Earlier versions of these stories have been published previously in *American Poetry Review, The American Voice, Harper's Magazine, Helicon, Missouri Review, North American Review, StoryQuarterly*; in *Five Pears or Peaches* (Broken Moon Press), *Slow Trains Overhead: Chicago Poems and Stories* (University of Chicago Press), and in the anthologies *Chicago Works* (Morton Press), *Vital Lines: Contemporary Fiction about Medicine* (St. Martin's Press); and have been broadcast on *This American Life*.

About the Author

Reginald Gibbons is the author of a novel, *Sweetbitter* (LSU Press); ten books of poems, most recently *Last Lake* (University of Chicago Press); a book about poetry, *How Poems Think* (University of Chicago Press); and many other works, including translations from Spanish and ancient Greek. His book *Creatures of a Day* (LSU Press) was a Finalist for the National Book Award in poetry. He taught for many years in the MFA Program for Writers at Warren Wilson College, and is Frances Hooper Professor of Arts and Humanities at Northwestern University. From 2012 to early 2017, he was one of many who participated in creating the American Writers Museum (Chicago). He was born and raised in Houston, where he studied piano and clarinet and was thrown by horses, and then studied Spanish and creative writing at Princeton, and creative writing and comparative literature at Stanford.

BOA Editions, Ltd. *American Reader Series*

No. 1   *Christmas at the Four Corners of the Earth*
Prose by Blaise Cendrars
Translated by Bertrand Mathieu

No. 2   *Pig Notes & Dumb Music: Prose on Poetry*
By William Heyen

No. 3   *After-Images: Autobiographical Sketches*
By W. D. Snodgrass

No. 4   *Walking Light: Memoirs and Essays on Poetry*
By Stephen Dunn

No. 5   *To Sound Like Yourself: Essays on Poetry*
By W. D. Snodgrass

No. 6   *You Alone Are Real to Me: Remembering Rainer Maria Rilke*
By Lou Andreas-Salomé

No. 7   *Breaking the Alabaster Jar: Conversations with Li-Young Lee*
Edited by Earl G. Ingersoll

No. 8   *I Carry A Hammer In My Pocket For Occasions Such As These*
By Anthony Tognazzini

No. 9   *Unlucky Lucky Days*
By Daniel Grandbois

No. 10   *Glass Grapes and Other Stories*
By Martha Ronk

No. 11   *Meat Eaters & Plant Eaters*
By Jessica Treat

No. 12   *On the Winding Stair*
By Joanna Howard

No. 13   *Cradle Book*
By Craig Morgan Teicher

No. 14   *In the Time of the Girls*
By Anne Germanacos

No. 15   *This New and Poisonous Air*
By Adam McOmber

No. 16   *To Assume a Pleasing Shape*
By Joseph Salvatore

No. 17   *The Innocent Party*
By Aimee Parkison

Colophon

BOA Editions, Ltd., a not-for-profit publisher of poetry and other literary works, fosters readership and appreciation of contemporary literature. By identifying, cultivating, and publishing both new and established poets and selecting authors of unique literary talent, BOA brings high-quality literature to the public. Support for this effort comes from the sale of its publications, grant funding, and private donations.

The publication of this book is made possible, in part, by the special support of the following individuals:

Anonymous x 3
Nin Andrews
Christopher & DeAnna Cebula
Gwen & Gary Conners
Gouvernet Arts Fund
Peg Heminway, *in honor of Grant Holcomb*
Sandi Henschel
Grant Holcomb
Christopher Kennedy
X. J. & Dorothy M. Kennedy
Jack & Gail Langerak
Deborah Ronnen & Sherman Levey
Peter Makuck
Robert & Francie Marx
Aimee Parkison, *in memory of Jim McGavran, a beloved professor of English for 41 years*
Boo Poulin
Steven O. Russell & Phyllis Rifkin-Russell
Susan & David Senise
Bernadette Weaver-Catalana